# MIGNON G. EBERHART,

whose *While the Patient Slept* won the Scotland Yard Prize, and whose books have sold over a quarter of a million copies in America alone, has in this book created another of her very clever and attractive amateur sleuths.

Susan Dare is a charming young writer of mystery stories who has long pursued clues on paper with relentless logic but who has never encountered an actual murder. Then came that eventful week at Christabel Frame's—where she first met Jim Byrne and first met murder. Red is the color of violent death, and a red stone enabled Susan to duplicate for the first time in the realm of true murder her many triumphs in the field of fictional crime.

Meeting Jim Byrne was a turning point in Susan's life. That resourceful young reporter had a faculty for being where things happened . . . before they happened. And because Jim had an unconcealed admiration for Susan she found herself involved in rapid order in the case of the monkey and the ventriloquist; the affair of the Easter Island devil and the frightened wife; the case of the calico dog; the mystery of the claret lipstick, and the secret of the tragic-eyed ballet dancer.

Mignon G. Eberhart is acknowledged to be one of America's finest writers of the mystery story. She has a world-wide following, and her novels have been translated into eight languages. Her books are distinguished for their style, their sureness of touch, atmosphere, ingenuity, and suspense. The strength and dexterity displayed in these Susan Dare stories mark them as some of her finest work.

# THE CASES OF SUSAN DARE

BOOKS BY
MIGNON G. EBERHART

The Cases of Susan Dare
The Dark Garden
The White Cockatoo
Murder by an Aristocrat
From This Dark Stairway
The Mystery of Hunting's End
While the Patient Slept
The Patient in Room 18

# THE CASES OF SUSAN DARE

### MIGNON G. EBERHART

The cases of the Calico Dog . . . the claret lipstick . . . the red stone . . . the secret of the tragic-eyed ballet dancer . . . the affairs of the ventriloquist and the monkey . . . and the Easter Island devil and the frightened wife.

Leyden, Mass. 01337

Republished 1975
By Special Arrangement
with Doubleday & Co.

*Mystery*
*Ebe*

**Library of Congress Cataloging in Publication Data**

Eberhart, Mignon Good, 1899-
   The cases of Susan Dare.

   Reprint of the 1934 ed. published by Doubleday for the Crime Club, New York.
   I. Title.
PZ3.E159Cas12   [PS3509.B453]     813'.5'2     75-29119

COPYRIGHT, 1934
BY MIGNON G. EBERHART
ALL RIGHTS RESERVED

FIRST EDITION

## CONTENTS

|  | PAGE |
|---|---|
| INTRODUCING SUSAN DARE | 1 |
| SPIDER | 51 |
| EASTER DEVIL | 98 |
| THE CLARET STICK | 147 |
| THE MAN WHO WAS MISSING | 200 |
| THE CALICO DOG | 253 |

# THE CASES OF SUSAN DARE

### Introducing Susan Dare

SUSAN DARE WATCHED a thin stream of blue smoke ascend without haste from the long throat of a tiger lily. Michela, then, had escaped also. She was not, however, on the long veranda, for the clear, broadening light of the rising moon revealed it wide and empty, and nothing moved against the silvered lawn which sloped gently toward the pine woods.

Susan listened a moment for the tap of Michela's heels, did not hear it or any other intrusive sound, and then pushed aside the bowl of lilies on the low window seat, let the velvet curtains fall behind her, and seated herself in the little niche thus formed. It was restful and soothing to be thus shut away from the house with its subtly warring elements and to make herself part of the silent night beyond the open windows.

A pity, thought Susan, to leave. But after tonight she could not stay. After all, a guest, any guest, ought to have sense enough to leave when a situation develops in the family of her hostess. The thin trail of smoke from the lily caught Susan's glance again and she wished Michela wouldn't amuse herself by putting cigarette ends in flowers.

A faint drift of voices came from somewhere, and Susan shrank farther into herself and into the tranquil night. It had been an unpleasant dinner, and there would be still an hour or so before she could gracefully extract herself and escape again. Nice of Christabel to give her the guest house—the small green cottage across the terrace at the other side of the house, and through the hedge and up the winding green path. Christabel Frame was a perfect hostess, and Susan had had a week of utter rest and content.

But then Randy Frame, Christabel's young brother, had returned.

And immediately Joe Bromfel and his wife Michela, guests also, had arrived, and with them something that had destroyed all content. The old house of the Frames, with its gracious pillars and long windows and generous dim spaces, was exactly the same—the lazy Southern air and the misty blue hills and the quiet pine woods and the boxed paths through the flowers—none of it had actually changed. But it was, all the same, a different place.

A voice beyond the green velvet curtains called impatiently: "Michela—Michela——"

It was Randy Frame. Susan did not move, and she was sure that the sweeping velvet curtains hid even her silver toes. He was probably at the door of the library, and she could see, without looking, his red hair and lithe young body and impatient, thin face. Impatient for Michela. Idiot, oh, idiot, thought Susan. Can't you see what you are doing to Christabel?

His feet made quick sounds upon the parquet floor of the hall and were gone, and Susan herself made a sharply impatient movement. Because the Frame men had been red-haired, gallant, quick-tempered, reckless, and (added Susan to the saga) abysmally stupid and selfish, Randy had accepted the mold without question. A few words from the dinner conversation floated back into Susan's memory. They'd been talking of fox hunting—a safe enough topic, one would have thought, in the Carolina hills. But talk had veered—through Michela, was it?—to a stableman who had been shot by one of the Frames and killed. It had happened a long time ago, had been all but forgotten, and had nothing at all to do with the present generation of Frames. But Christabel said hurriedly it had been an accident; dreadful. She had looked white. And Randy had laughed and said the Frames shot first and inquired afterwards and that there was always a revolver in the top buffet drawer.

"Here she is," said a voice. The curtains were pulled suddenly backward, and Randy, a little flushed, stood there. His face fell as he discovered Susan's fair, smooth hair and thin lace gown. "Oh," he said. "I thought you were Michela."

Others were trailing in from the hall, and a polite hour or so must be faced. Queer how suddenly and inexplicably things had become tight and strained and unpleasant!

Randy had turned away and vanished without more words, and Tryon Welles, strolling across the room with Christabel, was looking at Susan and smiling affably.

"Susan Dare," he said. "Watching the moonlight, quietly planning murder." He shook his head and turned to Christabel. "I simply don't believe you, Christabel. If this young woman writes anything, which I doubt, it's gentle little poems about roses and moonlight."

Christabel smiled faintly and sat down. Mars, his black face shining, was bringing in the coffee tray. In the doorway Joe Bromfel, dark and bulky and hot-looking in his dinner coat, lingered a moment to glance along the hall and then came into the room.

"If Susan writes poems," said Christabel lightly, "it is her secret. You are quite wrong, Tryon. She writes——" Christabel's silver voice hesitated. Her slender hands were searching, hovering rather blindly over the tray, the large amethyst on one white finger full of trembling purple lights. It was a barely perceptible second before she took a fragile old cup and began to pour from the tall silver coffee pot. "She writes murders," said Christabel steadily. "Lovely, grisly ones, with sensible solutions. Sugar, Tryon? I've forgotten."

"One. But isn't that for Miss Susan?"

Tryon Welles was still smiling. He, the latest arrival, was a neat gray man with tight eyes, pink cheeks, and an affable manner. The only obvious thing about him was a rather finical regard for color, for he wore gray tweed with exactly the right shades of green—green tie, green shirt, a cautious green stripe in gray socks. He had reached the house on the heels of his telephoned message from town, saying he had to talk business with Christabel, and he had not had time to dress before dinner.

"Coffee, Joe?" asked Christabel. She was very deft with the delicate china. Very deft and very graceful, and Susan could not imagine how she knew that Christabel's hands were shaking.

Joe Bromfel stirred, turned his heavy dark face toward the hall again, saw no one, and took coffee from Christabel's lovely hand. Christabel avoided looking directly into his face, as, Susan had noticed, she frequently did.

"A sensible solution," Tryon Welles was saying thoughtfully. "Do murders have sensible solutions?"

His question hung in the air. Christabel did not reply, and Joe Bromfel did not appear to hear it. Susan said:

"They must have. After all, people don't murder just—well, just to murder."

"Just for the fun of it, you mean?" said Tryon Welles, tasting his coffee. "No, I suppose not. Well, at any rate," he went on, "it's nice to know your interest in murder is not a practical one."

He probably thought he was making light and pleasant conversation, reflected Susan. Strange that he did not know that every time he said the word "murder" it fell like a heavy stone in that silent room. She was about to wrench the conversation to another channel when Michela and Randy entered from the hall; Randy was laughing and Michela smiling.

At the sound of Randy's laugh, Joe Bromfel twisted bulkily around to watch their approach, and, except for Randy's laugh, it was entirely silent in the long book-lined room. Susan watched too. Randy was holding Michela's hand, swinging it as if to suggest a kind of frank camaraderie. Probably, thought Susan, he's been kissing her out in the darkness of the garden. Holding her very tight.

Michela's eyelids were white and heavy over unexpectedly shallow dark eyes. Her straight black hair was parted in the middle and pulled severely backward to a knot on her rather fat white neck. Her mouth was deeply crimson. She had been born, Susan knew, in rural New England, christened Michela by a romantic mother, and had striven to live up to the name ever since. Or down, thought Susan tersely, and wished she could take young Randy by his large and outstanding ears and shake him.

Michela had turned toward a chair, and her bare back presented itself to Susan, and she saw the thin red line with an angle that a man's cuff, pressing into the creamy flesh, had made. It was unmistakable. Joe Bromfel had seen it, too. He couldn't have helped seeing it. Susan looked into her coffee cup and wished fervently that Joe Bromfel hadn't seen the imprint of Randy's cuff, and then wondered why she wished it so fervently.

"Coffee, Michela?" said Christabel, and something in her voice was more, all at once, than Susan could endure. She rose and said rather breathlessly:

"Christabel darling, do you mind—I have some writing to do——"

"Of course." Christabel hesitated. "But wait —I'll go along with you to the cottage."

"Don't let us keep you, Christabel," said Michela lazily.

Christabel turned to Tryon Welles and neatly forestalled a motion on his part to accompany her and Susan.

"I won't be long, Tryon," she said definitely. "When I come back—we'll talk."

A clear little picture etched itself on Susan's mind: the long, lovely room, the mellow little areas of light under lamps here and there, one falling directly upon the chair she had just left, the pools of shadows surrounding them; Michela's yellow satin, and Randy's red head and slim black shoulders; Joe, a heavy, silent figure, watching them broodingly; Tryon Welles, neat and gray and affable, and Christabel with her gleaming red head held high on her slender neck, walking lightly and gracefully amid soft mauve chiffons. Halfway across the room she paused to accept a cigarette from Tryon and to bend to the small flare of a lighter he held for her, and the amethyst on her finger caught the flickering light of it and shone.

Then Susan and Christabel had crossed the empty flagstone veranda and turned toward the terrace.

Their slippered feet made no sound upon the velvet grass. Above the lily pool the flower fragrances were sweet and heavy on the night air.

"Did you hear the bullfrog last night?" asked Christabel. "He seems to have taken up a permanent residence in the pool. I don't know what to do about him. Randy says he'll shoot him, but I don't want that. He *is* a nuisance of course, bellowing away half the night. But after all—even bullfrogs—have a right to live."

"Christabel," said Susan, trying not to be abrupt, "I must go soon. I have—work to do——"

Christabel stopped and turned to face her. They were at the gap in the laurel hedge where a path began and wound upward to the cottage.

"Don't make excuses, Susan honey," she said gently. "Is it the Bromfels?"

A sound checked Susan's reply—an unexpectedly eerie sound that was like a wail. It rose and swelled amid the moonlit hills, and Susan gasped and Christabel said quickly, though with a catch in her voice: "It's only the dogs howling at the moon."

"They are not," Susan said, "exactly cheerful. It emphasizes——" She checked herself abruptly on the verge of saying that it emphasized their isolation.

Christabel had turned in at the path. It was darker there, and her cigarette made a tiny red glow. "If Michela drops another cigarette into a flower I'll kill her," said Christabel quietly.

"*What*——"

"I said I'd kill her," said Christabel. "I won't, of course. But she—oh, you've seen how things are, Susan. You can't have failed to see. She took Joe—years ago. Now she's taking Randy."

Susan was thankful that she couldn't see Christabel's face. She said something about infatuation and Randy's youth.

"He is twenty-one," said Christabel. "He's no younger than I was when Joe—when Joe and I were to be married. That was why Michela was here—to be a guest at the wedding and all the parties." They walked on for a few quiet steps before Christabel added: "It was the day before the wedding that they left together."

Susan said: "Has Joe changed?"

"In looks, you mean," said Christabel, understanding. "I don't know. Perhaps. He must have changed inside. But I don't want to know that."

"Can't you send them away?"

"Randy would follow."

"Tryon Welles," suggested Susan desperately. "Maybe he could help. I don't know how, though. Talk to Randy, maybe."

Christabel shook her head.

"Randy wouldn't listen. Opposition makes him stubborn. Besides, he doesn't like Tryon. He's had to borrow too much money from him."

It wasn't like Christabel to be bitter. One of the dogs howled again and was joined by others. Susan shivered.

"You are cold," said Christabel. "Run along inside, and thanks for listening. And—I think you'd better go, honey. I meant to keep you for comfort. But——"

"No, no, I'll stay—I didn't know——"

"Don't be nervous about being alone. The dogs would know it if a stranger put a foot on the place. Good-night," said Christabel firmly, and was gone.

The guest cottage was snug and warm and tranquil, but Susan was obliged finally to read herself to sleep and derived only a small and fleeting satisfaction from the fact that it was over a rival author's book that she finally grew drowsy. She didn't sleep well even then, and was glad suddenly that she'd asked for the guest cottage and was alone and safe in that tiny retreat.

Morning was misty and chill.

It was perhaps nine-thirty when Susan opened the cottage door, saw that mist lay thick and white, and went back to get her rubbers. Tryon Welles, she thought momentarily, catching a glimpse of herself in the mirror, would have nothing at all that was florid and complimentary to say this morning. And indeed, in her brown knitted suit, with her fair hair tight and smooth and her spectacles on, she looked not unlike a chill and aloof little owl.

The path was wet, and the laurel leaves shining with moisture, and the hills were looming gray shapes. The house lay white and quiet, and she saw no one about.

It was just then that it came. A heavy concussion of sound, blanketed by mist.

Susan's first thought was that Randy had shot the bullfrog.

But the pool was just below her, and no one was there.

Besides, the sound came from the house. Her feet were heavy and slow in the drenched grass— the steps were slippery and the flagstones wet. Then she was inside.

The wide hall ran straight through the house, and away down at its end Susan saw Mars. He was running away from her, his black hands outflung, and she was vaguely conscious that he was shouting something. He vanished, and instinct drew Susan to the door at the left which led to the library.

She stopped, frozen, in the doorway.

Across the room, sagging bulkily over the arm of the green damask chair in which she'd sat the previous night, was a man. It was Joe Bromfel, and he'd been shot, and there was no doubt that he was dead.

A newspaper lay at his feet as if it had slipped there. The velvet curtains were pulled together across the window behind him.

Susan smoothed back her hair. She couldn't think at all, and she must have slipped down to the footstool near the door for she was there when Mars, his face drawn, and Randy, white as his pajamas, came running into the room. They were talking excitedly and were examining a revolver which Randy had picked up from the floor. Then Tryon Welles came from somewhere, stopped beside her, uttered an incredulous exclamation, and ran across the room too. Then Christabel came and stopped, too, on the threshold, and became under Susan's very eyes a different woman—a strange woman, shrunken and gray, who said in a dreadful voice:

"*Joe—Joe*——"

Only Susan heard or saw her. It was Michela, hurrying from the hall, who first voiced the question.

"I heard something—what was it? What——" She brushed past Christabel.

"*Don't look, Michela!*"

But Michela looked—steadily and long. Then her flat dark eyes went all around the room and she said: "Who shot him?"

For a moment there was utter shocked stillness.

Then Mars cleared his throat and spoke to Randy.

"I don' know who shot him, Mista Randy. But I saw him killed. An' I saw the han' that killed him——"

"*Hand!*" screamed Michela.

"Hush, Michela." Tryon Welles was speaking. "What do you mean, Mars?"

"They ain't nothin' to tell except that, Mista Tryon. I was just comin' to dust the library and was right there at the door when I heard the shot, and there was just a han' stickin' out of them velvet curtains. And I saw the han' and I saw the revolver and I—I do' know what I did then." Mars wiped his forehead. "I guess I ran for help, Mista Tryon."

There was another silence.

"Whose hand was it, Mars?" said Tryon Welles gently.

Mars blinked and looked very old.

"Mista Tryon, God's truth is, I do' know. I do' know."

Randy thrust himself forward.

"Was it a man's hand?"

"I reckon it was maybe," said the old Negro slowly, looking at the floor. "But I do' know for sure, Mista Randy. All I saw was—was the red ring on it."

"A red *ring?*" cried Michela. "What do you mean——"

Mars turned a bleak dark face toward Michela; a face that rejected her and all she had done to his house. "A red ring, Miz Bromfel," he said with a kind of dignity. "It sort of flashed. And it was red."

After a moment Randy uttered a curious laugh.

"But there's not a red ring in the house. None of us runs to rubies—" He stopped abruptly. "I say, Tryon, hadn't we better—well, carry him to the divan. It isn't decent to—just leave him—like that."

"I suppose so—" Tryon Welles moved toward the body. "Help me, Randy——"

The boy shivered, and Susan quite suddenly found her voice.

"Oh, but you can't do that. You can't——" She stopped. The two men were looking at her in astonishment. Michela, too, had turned toward her, although Christabel did not move.

"But you can't do that," repeated Susan. "Not when it's—murder."

This time the word, falling into the long room, was weighted with its own significance. Tryon Welles' gray shoulders moved.

"She's perfectly right," he said. "I'd forgotten—if I ever knew. But that's the way of it. We'll have to send for people—doctor, sheriff, coroner, I suppose."

Afterward, Susan realized that but for Tryon Welles the confusion would have become mad. He took a quiet command of the situation, sending Randy, white and sick-looking, to dress, telephoning into town, seeing that the body was decently covered, and even telling Mars to bring them hot coffee. He was here, there, everywhere:

upstairs, downstairs, seeing to them all, and finally outside to meet the sheriff . . . brisk, alert, efficient. In the interval Susan sat numbly beside Christabel on the love seat in the hall, with Michela restlessly prowling up and down the hall before their eyes, listening to the telephone calls, drinking hot coffee, watching everything with her sullen, flat black eyes. Her red-and-white sports suit, with its scarlet bracelets and earrings, looked garish and out of place in that house of violent death.

And Christabel. Still a frozen image of a woman who drank coffee automatically, she sat erect and still and did not speak. The glowing amethyst on her finger caught the light and was the only living thing about her.

Gradually the sense of numb shock and confusion was leaving Susan. Fright was still there and horror and a queer aching pity, but she saw Randy come running down the wide stairway again, his red hair smooth now above a sweater, and she realized clearly that he was no longer white and sick and frightened; he was instead alert and defiantly ready for what might come. And it would be, thought Susan, in all probability, plenty.

And it was.

Questions—questions. The doctor, who was kind, the coroner, who was not; the sheriff, who was merely observant—all of them questioning without end. No time to think. No time to comprehend. Time only to reply as best one might.

But gradually out of it all certain salient facts began to emerge. They were few, however, and brief.

The revolver was Randy's, and it had been taken from the top buffet drawer—when, no one knew or, at least, would tell. "Everybody knew it was there," said Randy sulkily. The fingerprints on it would probably prove to be Randy's and Mars's, since they picked it up.

No one knew anything of the murder, and no one had an alibi, except Liz (the Negro second girl) and Minnie (the cook), who were together in the kitchen.

Christabel had been writing letters in her own room: she'd heard the shot, but thought it was only Randy shooting a bullfrog in the pool. But then she'd heard Randy and Mars running down the front stairway, so she'd come down too. Just to be sure that that was what it was.

"What else did you think it could be?" asked

the sheriff. But Christabel said stiffly that she didn't know.

Randy had been asleep when Mars had awakened him. He had not heard the sound of the shot at all. He and Mars had hurried down to the library. (Mars, it developed, had gone upstairs by means of the small back stairway off the kitchen.)

Tryon Welles had walked down the hill in front of the house to the mail box and was returning when he heard the shot. But it was muffled, and he did not know what had happened until he reached the library. He created a mild sensation at that point by taking off a ring, holding it so they could all see it, and demanding of Mars if that was the ring he had seen on the murderer's hand. However, the sensation was only momentary, for the large clear stone was as green as his neat green tie.

"No, suh, Mista Tryon," said Mars. "The ring on the han' I saw was red. I could see it plain, an' it was red."

"This," said Tryon Welles, "is a flawed emerald. I asked because I seem to be about the only person here wearing a ring. But I suppose that, in justice to us, all our belongings should be searched."

Upon which the sheriff's gaze slid to the purple pool on Christabel's white hand. He said, however, gently, that that was being done, and would Mrs. Michela Bromfel tell what she knew of the murder.

But Mrs. Michela Bromfel somewhat spiritedly knew nothing of it. She'd been walking in the pine woods, she said defiantly, glancing obliquely at Randy, who suddenly flushed all over his thin face. She'd heard the shot but hadn't realized it was a gunshot. However, she was curious and came back to the house.

"The window behind the body opens toward the pine woods," said the sheriff. "Did you see anyone, Mrs. Bromfel?"

"No one at all," said Michela definitely.

Well, then, had she heard the dogs barking? The sheriff seemed to know that the kennels were just back of the pine woods.

But Michela had not heard the dogs.

Someone stirred restively at that, and the sheriff coughed and said unnecessarily that there was no tramp about, then, and the questioning continued. Continued wearily on and on and on, and still no one knew how Joe Bromfel had met his death. And as the sheriff was at last dismissing them and talking to the coroner of an inquest, one of his men came to report on the search. No one was in the house who didn't belong there; they could tell nothing of footprints; the French windows back of the body had been ajar, and there was no red ring anywhere in the house.

"Not, that is, that we can find," said the man.

"All right," said the sheriff. "That'll be all now, folks. But I'd take it kindly if you was to stay around here today."

All her life Susan was to remember that still, long day with a kind of sharp reality. It was, after those first moments when she'd felt so ill and shocked, weirdly natural, as if, one event having occurred, another was bound to follow, and then upon that one's heels another, and all of them quite in the logical order of things. Even the incident of the afternoon, so trivial in itself but later so significant, was as natural, as unsurprising as anything could be. And that was her meeting with Jim Byrne.

It happened at the end of the afternoon, long

and painful, which Susan spent with Christabel, knowing somehow that, under her frozen surface, Christabel was grateful for Susan's presence. But there were nameless things in the air between them which could be neither spoken of nor ignored, and Susan was relieved when Christabel at last took a sedative and, eventually, fell into a sleep that was no more still than Christabel waking had been.

There was no one to be seen when Susan tiptoed out of Christabel's room and down the stairway, although she heard voices from the closed door of the library.

Out the wide door at last and walking along the terrace above the lily pool, Susan took a long breath of the mist-laden air.

So this was murder. This was murder, and it happened to people one knew, and it did indescribable and horrible things to them. Frightened them first, perhaps. Fear of murder itself came first—simple, primitive fear of the unleashing of the beast. And then on its heels came more civilized fear, and that was fear of the law, and a scramble for safety.

She turned at the hedge and glanced backward. The house lay white and stately amid its gardens as it had lain for generations. But it was no longer tranquil—it was charged now with violence. With murder. And it remained dignified and stately and would cling, as Christabel would cling and had clung all those years, to its protective ritual.

Christabel: Had she killed him? Was that why she was so stricken and gray? Or was it because she knew that Randy had killed him? Or was it something else?

Susan did not see the man till she was almost upon him, and then she cried out involuntarily, though she as a rule was not at all nervous. He was sitting on the small porch of the cottage, hunched up with his hat over his eyes and his coat collar turned up, furiously scribbling on a pad of paper. He jumped up as he heard her breathless little cry and whirled to face her and took off his hat all in one motion.

"May I use your typewriter?" he said.

His eyes were extremely clear and blue and lively. His face was agreeably irregular in feature, with a mouth that laughed a great deal, a chin that took insolence from no man, and generous width of forehead. His hair was thinning but not yet showing gray and his hands were unexpectedly fine and beautiful. "Hard on the surface," thought Susan. "Terribly sensitive, really. Irish. What's he doing here?"

Aloud she said: "Yes."

"Good. Can't write fast enough and want to get this story off tonight. I've been waiting for you, you know. They told me you wrote things. My name's Byrne. James Byrne. I'm a reporter. Cover special stories. I'm taking a busman's holiday. I'm actually on a Chicago paper and down here for a vacation. I didn't expect a murder story to break."

Susan opened the door upon the small living room.

"The typewriter's there. Do you need paper? There's a stack beside it."

He fell upon the typewriter absorbedly, like a dog upon a bone. She watched him for a while, amazed at his speed and fluency and utter lack of hesitancy.

Presently she lighted the fire already laid in the tiny fireplace and sat there quietly, letting herself be soothed by the glow of the flames and the steady rhythm of the typewriter keys. And for the first time that day its experiences, noted and stored away in whatever place observations are stored, began to arouse and assort and arrange themselves and march in some sort of order through her conscious thoughts. But it was a dark and macabre procession, and it frightened Susan. She was relieved when Jim Byrne spoke.

"I say," he said suddenly, over the clicking keys, "I've got your name Louise Dare. Is that right?"

"Susan."

He looked at her. The clicking stopped.

"Susan. Susan Dare," he repeated thoughtfully. "I say, you can't be the Susan Dare that writes murder stories!"

"Yes," said Susan guardedly, "I can be that Susan Dare."

There was an expression of definite incredulity in his face. "But you——"

"If you say," observed Susan tensely, "that I don't look as if I wrote murder stories, you can't use my typewriter for your story."

"I suppose you are all tangled up in this mess," he said speculatively.

"Yes," said Susan, sober again. "And no," she added, looking at the fire.

"Don't commit yourself," said Jim Byrne dryly. "Don't say anything reckless."

"But I mean just that," said Susan. "I'm a guest here. A friend of Christabel Frame's. I didn't murder Joe Bromfel. And I don't care at all about the rest of the people here except that I wish I'd never seen them."

"But you do," said the reporter gently, "care a lot about Christabel Frame?"

"Yes," said Susan gravely.

"I've got all the dope, you know," said the reporter softly. "It wasn't hard to get. Everybody around here knows about the Frames. The thing I can't understand is why she shot Joe. It ought to have been Michela."

"*What*——" Susan's fingers were digging into the wicker arms of her chair, and her eyes strove frantically to plumb the clear blue eyes above the typewriter.

"I say, it ought to have been Michela. She's the girl who's making the trouble."

"But it wasn't—it couldn't—Christabel wouldn't——"

"Oh, yes, she could," said the reporter rather wearily. "All sorts of people could do the strangest things. Christabel could murder. But I can't see why she'd murder Joe and let Michela go scot-free."

"Michela," said Susan in a low voice, "would have a motive."

"Yes, she's got a motive. Get rid of a husband. But so had Randy Frame. Same one. And he's what the people around here call a Red Frame—impulsive, reckless, bred to a tradition of—violence."

"But Randy was asleep—upstairs——"

He interrupted her.

"Oh, yes, I know all that. And you were approaching the house from the terrace, and Tryon Welles had gone down after the mail, and Miss Christabel was writing letters upstairs, and Michela was walking in the pine woods. Not a damn alibi among you. The way the house and grounds are laid out, neither you nor Tryon Welles nor Michela would be visible to each other. And anyone could have escaped readily from the window and turned up innocently a moment later from the hall. I know all that. Who was behind the curtains?"

"A tramp—" attempted Susan in a small voice. "A burglar——"

"Burglar nothing," said Jim Byrne with scorn. "The dogs would have had hysterics. It was one of you. *Who?*"

"I don't know," said Susan. "*I don't know!*" Her voice was uneven, and she knew it and tried to steady it and clutched the chair arms tighter. Jim Byrne knew it, too, and was suddenly alarmed.

"Oh, look here, now," he cried. "Don't look like that. Don't cry. Don't——"

"I am not crying," said Susan. "But it wasn't Christabel."

"You mean," said the reporter kindly, "that you don't want it to be Christabel. Well——" He glanced at his watch, said, "Golly," and flung his papers together and rose. "There's something I'll do. Not for you exactly—just for—oh, because. I'll let part of my story wait until tomorrow if you want the chance to try to prove your Christabel didn't murder him."

Susan was frowning perplexedly.

"You don't understand me," said the reporter cheerfully. "It's this. You write murder mysteries, and I've read one or two of them. They are not bad," he interpolated hastily, watching Susan. "Now, here's your chance to try a real murder mystery."

"*But I don't want*——" began Susan.

He checked her imperatively.

"You do want to," he said. "In fact, you've

got to. You see—your Christabel is in a spot. You know that ring she wears——"

"When did you see it?"

"Oh, does it matter?" he cried impatiently. "Reporters see everything. The point is the ring."

"But it's an amethyst," said Susan defensively.

"Yes," he agreed grimly. "It's an amethyst. And Mars saw a red stone. He saw it, it has developed, on the right hand. And the hand holding the revolver. And Christabel wears her ring on her right hand."

"But," repeated Susan. "It *is* an amethyst."

"M-m," said the reporter. "It's an amethyst. And a little while ago I said to Mars: 'What's the name of that flowering vine over there?' And he said: 'That red flower, suh? That's wisteria.'"

He paused. Susan felt exactly as if something had clutched her heart and squeezed it.

"The flowers were purple, of course," said the reporter softly. "The color of a dark amethyst."

"But he would have recognized Christabel's ring," said Susan after a moment.

"Maybe," said the reporter. "And maybe he

wishes he'd never said a word about the red ring. He was scared when he first mentioned it, probably; hadn't had a chance to think it over."

"But Mars—Mars would confess to murdering rather than——"

"No," said Jim Byrne soberly. "He wouldn't. That theory sounds all right. But it doesn't happen that way. People don't murder or confess to having murdered for somebody else. When it is a deliberate, planned murder and not a crazy drunken brawl, when anything can happen, there's a motive. And it's a strong and urgent and deeply personal and selfish motive and don't you forget it. I've got to hurry. Now then, shall I send in my story about the wisteria——"

"Don't," said Susan choking. "Oh, don't. Not yet."

He picked up his hat. "Thanks for the typewriter. Get your wits together and go to work. After all, you ought to know something of murders. I'll be seeing you."

The door closed, and the flames crackled. After a long time Susan moved to the writing table and drew a sheet of yellow manuscript paper toward her, and a pencil, and wrote: Characters; possible motives; clues; queries.

It was strange, she thought, not how different real life was to its written imitation, but how like. How terribly like!

She was still bent over the yellow paper when a peremptory knock at the door sent her pencil jabbing furiously on the paper and her heart into her throat. It proved to be, however, only Michela Bromfel, and she wanted help.

"It's my knees," said Michela irritably. "Christabel's asleep or something, and those coons in the kitchen are scared of their shadows." She paused to dig savagely at first one knee and then the other. "Have you got anything to put on my legs? I'm nearly going crazy. It's not mosquito bites. I don't know what it is. Look!"

She sat down, pulled back her white skirt and rolled down her thin stockings, disclosing just above each knee a scarlet blotchy rim around her fat white legs.

Susan looked and had to resist a wild desire to giggle. "It's n-nothing," she said, quivering. "That is, it's only jiggers—here, I'll get you something. Alcohol."

"Jiggers," said Michela blankly. "What's that?"

Susan went into the bathroom. "Little bugs,"

she called. Where was the alcohol? "They are thick in the pine woods. It'll be all right by morning." Here it was. She took the bottle in her hand and turned again through the bedroom into the tiny living room.

At the door she stopped abruptly. Michela was standing at the writing table. She looked up, saw Susan, and her flat dark eyes flickered.

"Oh," said Michela. "Writing a story?"

"No," said Susan. "It's not a story. Here's the alcohol."

Under Susan's straight look Michela had the grace to depart rather hastily, yanking up her stockings and twisting them hurriedly, and clutching at the bottle of alcohol. Her red bracelets clanked, and her scarlet fingernails looked as if they'd been dipped in blood. Of the few people who might have killed Joe Bromfel, Susan reflected coolly, she would prefer it to be Michela.

It was just then that a curious vagrant memory began to tease Susan. Rather it was not so much a memory as a memory *of* a memory—something that sometime she had known and now could not remember. It was tantalizing. It was maddeningly elusive. It floated teasingly on the very edge of her consciousness.

Deliberately, at last, Susan pushed it away and went back to work. Christabel and the amethyst. Christabel and the wisteria. Christabel.

It was dark and still drizzly when Susan took her way down toward the big house.

At the laurel hedge she met Tryon Welles.

"Oh, hello," he said. "Where've you been?"

"At the cottage," said Susan. "There was nothing I could do. How's Christabel?"

"Liz says she is still asleep—thank heaven for that. God, what a day! You oughtn't to be prowling around alone at this time of night. I'll walk to the house with you."

"Have the sheriff and other men gone?"

"For the time being. They'll be back, I suppose."

"Do they know any more about—who killed him?"

"I don't know. You can't tell much. I don't know of any evidence they have unearthed. They asked me to stay on." He took a quick puff or two of his cigarette and then said irritably: "It puts me in a bad place. It's a business deal where time matters. I'm a broker—I ought to be going back to New York tonight——" He broke off abruptly and said: "Oh, Randy—" as young

Randy's pale, thin face above a shining mackintosh emerged from the dusk—"let's just escort Miss Susan to the steps."

"Is she afraid of the famous tramp?" asked Randy and laughed unpleasantly. He'd been drinking, thought Susan, with a flicker of anxiety. Sober, Randy was incalculable enough; drinking, he might be dangerous. Could she do anything with him? No, better leave it to Tryon Welles. "The tramp," Randy was repeating loudly. "Don't be afraid of a tramp. It wasn't any tramp killed Joe. And everybody knows it. You're safe enough, Susan, unless you've got some evidence. Have you got any evidence, Susan?"

He took her elbow and joggled it urgently.

"She's the quiet kind, Tryon, that sees everything and says nothing. Bet she's got evidence enough to hang us all. Evidence. That's what we need. Evidence."

"Randy, you're drunk," said Susan crisply. She shook off his clutch upon her arm and then, looking at his thin face, which was so white and tight-drawn in the dusk, was suddenly sorry for him. "Go on and take your walk," she said more kindly. "Things will be all right."

"Things will never be the same again," said Randy. "Never the same—do you know why, Susan?" He's very drunk, thought Susan; worse than I thought. "It's because Michela shot him. Yes, sir."

"Randy, shut up!"

"Don't bother me, Tryon, I know what I'm saying. And Michela," asserted Randy with simplicity, "makes me sick."

"Come on, Randy." This time Tryon Welles took Randy's arm. "I'll take care of him, Miss Susan."

The house was deserted and seemed cold. Christabel was still asleep, Michela nowhere to be seen, and Susan finally told Mars to send her dinner on a tray to the cottage and returned quietly like a small brown wraith through the moist twilight.

But she was an oddly frightened wraith.

She was alone on the silent terrace, she was alone on the dark path—strange that she felt as if someone else was there, too. Was the bare fact of murder like a presence hovering, beating dark wings, waiting to sweep downward again?

"Nonsense," said Susan aloud. "Nonsense——" and ran the rest of the way.

She was not, however, to be alone in the cottage, for Michela sat there, composedly awaiting her.

"Do you mind," said Michela, "if I spend the night here? There's two beds in there. You see—" she hesitated, her flat dark eyes were furtive—"I'm—afraid."

"Of what?" said Susan, after a moment. "Of whom?"

"I don't know who," said Michela, "or what."

After a long, singularly still moment Susan forced herself to say evenly:

"Stay if you are nervous. It's safe here." Was it? Susan continued hurriedly: "Mars will send up dinner."

Michela's thick white hand made an impatient movement.

"Call it nerves—although I've not a nerve in my body. But when Mars comes with dinner— just be sure it *is* Mars before you open the door, will you? Although as to that— *I* don't know. But I brought my revolver—loaded." She reached into her pocket, and Susan sat upright, abruptly. Susan, whose knowledge of revolvers had such a wide and peculiar range that any policeman, learning of it, would arrest her on suspicion alone, was nevertheless somewhat uneasy in their immediate vicinity.

"Afraid?" said Michela.

"Not at all," said Susan. "But I don't think a revolver will be necessary."

"I hope not, I'm sure," said Michela somberly and stared at the fire.

After that, as Susan later reflected, there was not much to be said. The only interruption during the whole queer evening was the arrival of Mars and dinner.

Later in the evening Michela spoke again, abruptly. "I didn't kill Joe," she said. And after another long silence she said unexpectedly: "Did Christabel ask you how to kill him and get by with it?"

"*No!*"

"Oh." Michela looked at her queerly. "I thought maybe she'd got you to plan it for her. You—knowing so much about murders and all."

"She didn't," said Susan forcefully. "And I don't plan murders for my friends, I assure you. I'm going to bed."

Michela, following her, put the revolver on the small table between the two beds.

If the night before had been heavy with

apprehension, this night was an active nightmare. Susan tossed and turned and was uneasily conscious that Michela was awake and restless, too.

Susan must have slept at last, though, for she waked up with a start and sat upright, instantly aware of some movement in the room. Then she saw a figure dimly outlined against the window. It was Michela.

Susan joined her. "What are you doing?"

"Hush," whispered Michela. Her face was pressed against the glass. Susan looked, too, but could see only blackness.

"There's someone out there," whispered Michela. "And if he moves again I'm going to shoot."

Susan was suddenly aware that the ice-cold thing against her arm was the revolver.

"You are not," said Susan and wrenched the thing out of Michela's hand. Michela gasped and whirled, and Susan said grimly: "Go back to bed. Nobody's out there."

"How do you know?" said Michela, her voice sulky.

"I don't," said Susan, very much astonished at herself, but clutching the revolver firmly.

"But I do know that you aren't going to start shooting. If there's any shooting to be done," said Susan with aplomb, "I'll do it myself. Go to bed."

But long after Michela was quiet Susan still sat bolt upright, clutching the revolver and listening.

Along toward dawn, out of the mêlée of confused, unhappy thoughts, the vagrant little recollection of a recollection came back to tantalize her. Something she'd known and now did not know. This time she returned as completely as she could over the track her thoughts had taken in the hope of capturing it by association. She'd been thinking of the murder and of the possible suspects; that if Michela had not murdered Joe, then there were left Randy and Christabel and Tryon Welles. And she didn't want it to be Christabel; it must not be Christabel. And that left Randy and Tryon Welles. Randy had a motive, but Tryon Welles had not. Tryon Welles wore a ring habitually, and Randy did not. But the ring was an emerald. And Christabel's ring was what Mars called red. Red—then what would he have called Michela's scarlet bracelet? Pink? But that was a bracelet. She wrenched herself back to dig at the troublesome phantom of a memory. It was something trivial—but something she could not project into her conscious memory. And it was something that somehow she needed. Needed now.

She awoke and was horrified to discover her cheek pillowed cosily upon the revolver. She thrust it away. And realized with a sinking of her heart that day had come and, with it, urgent problems. Christabel, first.

Michela was still silent and sulky. Crossing the terrace, Susan looked at the wisteria winding upward over its trellis. It was heavy with purple blossoms—purple like dark amethysts.

Christabel was in her own room, holding a breakfast tray on her lap and looking out the window with a blank, unseeing gaze. She was years older; shrunken somehow inside. She was pathetically willing to answer the few questions that Susan asked, but added nothing to Susan's small store of knowledge. She left her finally, feeling that Christabel wanted only solitude. But she went away reluctantly. It would not be long before Jim Byrne returned, and she had nothing to tell him—nothing, that is, except surmise.

Randy was not at breakfast, and it was a dark and uncomfortable meal. Dark because Tryon Welles said something about a headache and turned out the electric light, and uncomfortable because it could not be otherwise. Michela had changed to a thin suit—red again. The teasing ghost of a memory drifted over Susan's mind and away again before she could grasp it.

As the meal ended Susan was called to the telephone. It was Jim Byrne saying that he would be there in an hour.

On the terrace Tryon Welles overtook her again and said: "How's Christabel?"

"I don't know," said Susan slowly. "She looks—stunned."

"I wish I could make it easier for her," he said. "But—I'm caught, too. There's nothing I can do, really. I mean about the house, of course. Didn't she tell you?"

"No."

He looked at her, considered, and went on slowly.

"She wouldn't mind your knowing. You see— oh, it's tragically simple. But I can't help myself. It's like this: Randy borrowed money of me—kept on borrowing it, spent it like water.

Without Christabel knowing it, he put up the house and grounds as collateral. She knows now, of course. Now I'm in a pinch in business and have got to take the house over legally in order to borrow enough money on it myself to keep things going for a few months. Do you see?"

Susan nodded. Was it this knowledge, then, that had so stricken Christabel?

"I hate it," said Tryon Welles. "But what can I do? And now Joe's—death—on top of it—" he paused, reached absently for a cigarette case, extracted a cigarette, and the small flame from his lighter flared suddenly clear and bright. "It's—hell," he said, puffing, "for her. But what can I do? I've got my own business to save."

"I see," said Susan slowly.

And quite suddenly, looking at the lighter, she did see. It was as simple, as miraculously simple as that. She said, her voice to her own ears marvelously unshaken and calm: "May I have a cigarette?"

He was embarrassed at not having offered it to her: he fumbled for his cigarette case and then held the flame of the lighter for her. Susan was very deliberate about getting her cigarette lighted. Finally she did so, said, "Thank you," and added, quite as if she had the whole thing planned: "Will you wake Randy, Mr. Welles, and send him to me? Now?"

"Why, of course," he said. "You'll be in the cottage?"

"Yes," said Susan and fled.

She was bent over the yellow paper when Jim Byrne arrived.

He was fresh and alert and, Susan could see, prepared to be kind. He expected her, then, to fail.

"Well," he said gently, "have you discovered the murderer?"

"Yes," said Susan Dare.

Jim Byrne sat down quite suddenly.

"I know who killed him," she said simply, "but I don't know why."

Jim Byrne reached into his pocket for a handkerchief and dabbed it lightly to his forehead. "Suppose," he suggested in a hushed way, "you tell all."

"Randy will be here in a moment," said Susan. "But it's all very simple. You see, the final clue was only the proof. I knew Christabel couldn't have killed him, for two reasons: one is, she's inherently incapable of killing anything;

the other is—she loved him still. And I knew it wasn't Michela, because she is, actually, cowardly; and then, too, Michela had an alibi."

"Alibi?"

"She really *was* in the pine woods for a long time that morning. Waiting, I think, for Randy, who slept late. I know she was there, because she was simply chewed by jiggers, and they are only in the pine woods."

"Maybe she was there the day before?"

Susan shook her head decidedly.

"No, I know jiggers. If it had been during the previous day they'd have stopped itching by the time she came to me. And it wasn't during the afternoon, for no one went in the pine woods then except the sheriff's men."

"That would leave, then, Randy and Tryon Welles."

"Yes," said Susan. Now that it had come to doing it, she felt ill and weak; would it be her evidence, her words, that would send a fellow creature over that long and ignominious road that ends so tragically?

Jim Byrne knew what she was thinking.

"Remember Christabel," he said quietly.

"Oh, I know," said Susan sadly. She locked

her fingers together, and there were quick footsteps on the porch.

"You want me, Susan?" said Randy.

"Yes, Randy," said Susan. "I want you to tell me if you owed Joe Bromfel anything. Money—or—or anything."

"How did you know?" said Randy.

"Did you give him a note—anything?"

"Yes."

"What was your collateral?"

"The house—it's all mine——"

"When was it dated? Answer me, Randy."

He flung up his head.

"I suppose you've been talking to Tryon," he said defiantly. "Well, it was dated before Tryon got his note. I couldn't help it. I'd got some stocks on margin. I had to have——"

"So the house actually belonged to Joe Bromfel?" Susan was curiously cold. Christabel's house. Christabel's brother.

"Well, yes—if you want to put it like that."

Jim Byrne had risen quietly.

"And after Joe Bromfel, to Michela, if she knows of this and claims it?" pressed Susan.

"I don't know," said Randy. "I never thought of that."

Jim Byrne started to speak, but Susan silenced him.

"No, he really didn't think of it," she said wearily. "And I knew it wasn't Randy who killed him because he didn't, really, care enough for Michela to do that. It was—Tryon Welles who killed Joe Bromfel. He had to. For he had to silence Joe and then secure the note and, probably, destroy it, in order to have a clear title to the house, himself. Randy—did Joe have the note here with him?"

"Yes."

"It was not found upon his body?"

It was Jim Byrne who answered: "Nothing of the kind was found anywhere."

"Then," said Susan, "after the murder was discovered and before the sheriff arrived and the search began, only you and Tryon Welles were upstairs and had the opportunity to search Joe's room and find the note and destroy it. Was it you who did that, Randy?"

"*No—no!*" The color rose in his face.

"Then it must have been then that Tryon Welles found and destroyed it." She frowned. "Somehow, he must have known it was there. I don't know how—perhaps he had had words with Joe about it before he shot him and Joe inadvertently told him where it was. There was no time for him to search the body. But he knew——"

"Maybe," said Randy reluctantly, "I told him. You see—I knew Joe had it in his letter case. He—he told me. But I never thought of taking it."

"It was not on record?" asked Jim Byrne.

"No," said Randy, flushing. "I—asked him to keep it quiet."

"I wonder," said Susan, looking away from Randy's miserable young face, "just how Tryon Welles expected to silence you."

"Well," said Randy dully, after a moment, "it was not exactly to my credit. But you needn't rub it in. I never thought of this—I was thinking of—Michela. That she did it. I've had my lesson. And if he destroyed the note, how are you going to prove all this?"

"By your testimony," said Susan. "And besides—there's the ring."

"Ring," said Randy. Jim Byrne leaned forward intently.

"Yes," said Susan. "I'd forgotten. But I remembered that Joe had been reading the newspaper when he was killed. The curtains were pulled together back of him, so, in order to see the paper, he must have had the light turned on above his chair. It wasn't burning when I entered the library, or I should have noted it. So the murderer had pulled the cord of the lamp before he escaped. And ever since then he has been very careful to avoid any artificial light."

"What are you talking about?" cried Randy.

"Yet he had to keep on wearing the ring," said Susan. "Fortunately for him he didn't have it on the first night—I suppose the color at night would have been wrong with his green tie. But this morning he lit a cigarette and I saw."

"Saw what, in God's name," said Randy burstingly.

"That the stone isn't an emerald at all," replied Susan. "It's an Alexandrite. It changed color under the flare of the lighter."

"Alexandrite!" cried Randy impatiently. "What's that?"

"It's a stone that's a kind of red-purple under artificial light and green in daylight," said Jim Byrne shortly. "I had forgotten there was such a thing—I don't think I've ever happened to see one. They are rare—and costly. Costly," repeated Jim Byrne slowly. "This one has cost a life——"

Randy interrupted: "But if Michela knows about the note, why, Tryon may kill her——" He stopped abruptly, thought for a second or two, then got out a cigarette. "Let him," he said airily.

It had been Tryon Welles, then, prowling about during the night—if it had been anyone. He had been uncertain, perhaps, of the extent of Michela's knowledge—but certain of his ability to deal with her and with Randy, who was so heavily in his debt.

"Michela doesn't know now," said Susan slowly. "And when you tell her, Randy—she might settle for a cash consideration. And, Randy Frame, somehow you've got to recover this house for Christabel and do it honestly."

"But right now," said Jim Byrne cheerily. "For the sheriff. And my story."

At the doorway he paused to look at Susan. "May I come back later," he said, "and use your typewriter?"

"Yes," said Susan Dare.

### Spider

"BUT IT IS FANTASTIC," said Susan Dare, clutching the telephone. "You can't just be afraid. You've got to be afraid of something." She waited, but there was no reply.

"You mean," she said presently, in a hushed voice, "that I'm to go to this perfectly strange house, to be the guest of a perfectly strange woman——"

"To you," said Jim Byrne. "Not, I tell you, to me."

"But you said you had never seen her——"

"Don't maunder," said Jim Byrne sharply. "Of course I've never seen her. Now, Susan, do try to get this straight. This woman is Caroline Wray. One of the Wrays."

"Perfectly clear," said Susan. "Therefore I'm to go to her house and see why she's got an attack of nerves. Take a bag and prepare to spend the next few days as her guest. I'm sorry, Jim, but I'm busy. I've got to do a murder story this week and——"

"Sue," said Jim, "I'm serious."

Susan paused abruptly. He *was* serious.

"It's—I don't know how to explain it, Susan," he said. "It's just—well, I'm Irish, you know. And I'm—fey. Don't laugh."

"I'm not laughing," said Susan. "Tell me exactly what you want me to do."

"Just—watch things. There ought not to be any danger—don't see how there could be. To you."

Susan realized that she was going. "How many Wrays are there, and what do you think is going to happen?"

"There are four Wrays. But I don't know what is going on that has got Caroline so terrified. It was that—the terror in her voice—that made me call you."

"What's the number of the house?" said Susan.

He told her. "It's away north," he said. "One of those old houses—narrow, tall, hasn't changed, I suppose, since old Ephineas Wray died. He was a close friend, you know, of my father's. Don't know why Caroline called me: I suppose some vague notion that a man on a newspaper would know what to do. Now let me see—there's Caroline. She's the daughter of

Ephineas Wray. David is his grandson and Caroline's nephew and the only man—except the houseman—in the place. He's young—in his twenties, I believe. His father and mother died when he was a child."

"You mean there are three women?"

"Naturally. There's Marie—she is old Wray's adopted daughter—not born a Wray, but more like him than the rest of them. And Jessica—she's Caroline's cousin; but she's always lived with the Wrays because her father died young. People always assume that the three women are sisters. Actually, of course, they are not. But old Ephineas Wray left his fortune divided equally among them."

"And they all live there together?"

"Yes. David's not married."

"Is that," said Susan, at the note of finality in his voice, "all you know about them?"

"Absolutely everything. Not much for you to go on, is it? It was just," said Jim Byrne soberly, with the effect of a complete explanation, "that she was so—so horribly scared. Old Caroline, I mean."

Susan retraced the address slowly before she said again: "What was she afraid of?"

"I don't know," said Jim Byrne. "And—it's queer—but I don't think she knew either."

It was approaching five o'clock, with a dark fog rolling up from the lake and blending itself with the early winter twilight, when Susan Dare pressed the bell beside the wide old door—pressed it and waited. Lights were on in the street, but the house before her was dark, its windows curtained. The door was heavy and secretive.

But they were expecting her—or at least Caroline Wray was; it had all been arranged by telephone. Susan wondered what Caroline had told them; what Jim Byrne had told Caroline to say to explain her presence; and, suddenly, what Caroline was like.

"*Little Johnny hung his sister.*
*She was dead before they missed her.*
*Johnny's always up to tricks,*
*Ain't he cute, and only six——*"

The jingle had been haunting her with the persistency of a popular dance tune, and it gave accent to the impatient little beat of her brown oxford upon the stone step. Then a light flashed on above the door. Susan took a deep breath of the moist cold air and felt a sudden tightening of her nerves. The door was going to open.

It swung wider, and a warm current of air struck Susan's cheeks. Beyond was a dimly lit hall and a woman's figure—a tall, corseted figure with full sweeping skirts.

"Yes?" said a voice harshly out of the dimness.

"I am Susan Dare," said Susan.

"Oh—oh, yes." The figure moved aside and the door opened wider. "Come in, Miss Dare. We were expecting you."

Afterward Susan remembered her own hesitation on the dark threshold as the door closed with finality behind her, and the woman turned.

"I am Miss Jessica Wray," she said.

Jessica. This was the cousin, then.

She was a tall woman, large-boned, with a heavy, dark face, thick, iron-gray hair done high and full on her head, and long, strong hands. She was dressed after a much earlier fashion; one which, indeed, Susan was unable to date.

"We were expecting you," she said. "Caroline,

however, was obliged to go out." She paused just under the light and beside a long mirror.

Susan had a confused impression of the house, in that moment; an impression of old, crowded elegance. The mirror was wavery and framed in wide gilt; there were ferns in great marble urns; there were marble figures.

"We'll go up to your room," said Jessica. "Caroline said you would be in Chicago for several days. This way. You can leave your bag here. James will take it up later; he is out just now."

Susan put down her small suitcase, and followed Jessica. The newel post and stair rail were heavy and carved. The steps were carpeted and thickly padded. And the house was utterly, completely still. As they ascended the quiet stairs it grew increasingly hot and airless.

At the top of the stairs Jessica turned with a rigid motion of her strong body.

"Will you wait here a moment?" she said. "I'm not sure which room——"

Susan made some assenting gesture, and Jessica turned along the passage which ran toward the rear of the house.

So terrifically hot the house was. So crowded

with old and almost sentient furniture. So very silent.

Susan moved a bit restively. It was not a pleasant house. But Caroline had to be afraid of something—not just silence and heat and brooding, secretive old walls. She glanced down the length of hall, moved again to put her hand upon the tall newel post of the stair rail beside her. The carved top of it seemed to shift and move slightly under the pressure of her hand and confirmed in the strangest way her feeling that the house itself had a singular kind of life.

Then she was staring straight ahead of her through an open, lighted doorway. Beyond it was a large room, half bedroom and half sitting room. A lamp on a table cast a circle of light, and beside the table, silhouetted against the light, sat a woman with a book in her lap.

It must be Marie Wray—the older sister; the adopted Wray who was more like old Ephineas Wray than any of them.

Her face was in shadow with the light beyond it, so Susan could see only a blunt, fleshy white profile and a tight knot of shining black hair above a massive black silk bosom. She did not, apparently, know of Susan's presence, for she did not turn. There was a kind of patience about that massive, relaxed figure; a waiting. An enormous black female spider waiting in a web of shadows. But waiting for what? The suggestion was not one calculated to relieve the growing tension of Susan's nerves. The heat was making her dizzy; fanciful. Calling a harmless old woman a black spider merely because she was wearing a shiny black silk dress! Marie Wray still, so far as Susan could see, did not look at her, but there was suddenly the flicker of a motion on the table.

Susan looked and caught her breath in an incredulous little gasp.

There was actually a small gray creature on that table, directly under the lamplight. A small gray creature with a long tail. It sat down nonchalantly, pulled the lid off a box and dug its tiny hands into the box.

"It's a monkey," thought Susan with something like a clutch of hysteria. "It's a monkey—a spider monkey, is it?—with that tiny face."

It was turning its face jerkily about the room, peering with bright, anxious eyes here and there, and busily, furiously eating candy. It failed somehow to see Susan; or perhaps she was too far away to interest it. There was suddenly something curiously unreal about the scene. That, thought Susan, or the heat in this fantastic house, and turned at the approaching rustle of skirts down the passage. It was Jessica, and she looked at Susan and then through the open doorway and smiled coldly.

"Marie is deaf," she said. "I suppose she didn't realize you were here."

"No," said Susan.

"I'll tell her——" She made a stiff gesture with her long hand and turned to enter the room beyond the open door. As her gray silk rustled through the door the little monkey jerked around, gave her one piercing black glance and was gone from the table in a swift gray streak. He fled across the room, darted under an old sofa.

But Jessica did not reprove him. "Marie," she said loudly and distinctly.

There was a pause. Jessica's flowing gray silk skirts were now silhouetted against the table lamp, and the monkey absently began to lick its paw.

"Yes, Jessica." The voice was that of a person long deaf—entirely without tone.

"Susan Dare is here—you know—the daughter of Caroline's friend. Do you want to see her?"

"See her? No. No, not now. Later."

"Very well. Do you want anything?"

"No."

"Your cushions?"

Jessica's rigid back bent over Marie as she arranged a cushion. Then she turned and walked again toward Susan. Susan felt queerly fascinated and somehow oddly shocked to note that, as Jessica turned her rigid back to the room, the monkey darted out from under the sofa and was suddenly skittering across the room again in the direction of the table and the candy.

He would be, thought Susan, one very sick monkey. The house was too hot, and yet Susan shivered a bit. Why did people keep monkeys?

"This way," said Jessica firmly, and Susan preceded her down the hall and into exactly the kind of bedroom she might have expected it to be.

But Jessica did not intend to leave her alone to explore its Victorian fastnesses. Under her somewhat unnerving dark gaze, Susan removed her cock-eyed little hat, smoothed back her light hair and put her coat across a chair, only to have it placed immediately by Jessica in the enormous gloomy wardrobe. The servants, said Jessica, were out; the second girl and James because it was their half day out, the cook to do an errand.

"You are younger than I should have expected," she said abruptly to Susan. "Shall we go down now?"

As they passed down the stairs to the drawing room, a clock somewhere struck slowly, with long trembling variations.

"Five," said Jessica. "Caroline ought to return very soon. And David. He usually reaches home shortly after five. That is, if it isn't rainy. Traffic sometimes delays him. But it isn't rainy tonight!"

"Foggy," said Susan and obeyed the motion of Jessica's long gray hand toward a chair. It was not, however, a comfortable chair. And neither were the moments that followed comfortable, for Jessica sat sternly erect in a chair opposite Susan, folded her hands firmly in her silk lap and said exactly nothing. Susan started to speak a time or two, thought better of it, and herself sat in rather rigid silence. And was suddenly aware that she was acutely receptive to sight and sound and feeling.

It was not a pleasant sensation.

For she felt queerly as if the lives that were living themselves out in that narrow old house were pressing in upon her—as if long-spoken words and long-stifled whispers were living yet in the heated air.

She stirred restively and tried not to think of Marie Wray. Queer how difficult it was, once having seen Marie and heard her speak, not to think of that brooding figure—sitting in its web of shadows, waiting.

Three old women living in an old house. What were their relations to one another? Two of them she had seen and had heard speak, and knew no more of them than she had known. What about Caroline—the one who was afraid? She stirred again and knew Jessica was watching her.

They heard the bell, although it rang in some back part of the house. Jessica looked satisfied and rose.

"It's David," she said. At the door into the hall she added in a different tone: "And I suppose Caroline, too."

Susan knew she was tense. Yet there was nothing in that house for her—Susan Dare—to fear. It was Caroline who was afraid.

Then another woman stood in the doorway. Caroline, no doubt. A tall slender woman, a blonde who had faded into tremulous, wispy uncertainty. She did not speak. Her eyes were large and blue and feverish, and two bright pink spots fluttered in her thin cheeks, and her bare thin hands moved. Susan rose and went to her and took the two hands.

"But you're so young," said Caroline. Disappointment throbbed in her voice.

"I'm not really," said Susan.

"And so little——" breathed Caroline.

"But that doesn't matter at all," said Susan, speaking slowly, as one does to a nervous child. There were voices in the hall, but she was mainly aware of Caroline.

"No, I suppose not," said Caroline, finally looking into Susan's eyes. Terrified, Jim had said. Curious how right Jim managed to be.

Caroline's eyes sought into Susan's, and she was about to speak when there was a rustle in the doorway. Caroline's uncertain lips closed in a kind of gasp, and Jessica swept into the room.

"But I must know what she's afraid of," thought Susan. "I must get her alone—away from Jessica."

"Take off your coat, Caroline," said Jessica. "Don't stand there. I see you've spoken to Susan Dare. Put away your hat and coat and then come down again."

"Yes, Jessica," said Caroline. Her hands were moving again, and she looked away.

"Go on," said Jessica. Her voice was not sharp, it was merely undefeatable.

"Yes, Jessica," said Caroline.

"Marie is reading," said Jessica. "You needn't speak to her now unless you wish to do so. You may take Susan Dare in to see her later."

"Yes, Jessica."

Caroline disappeared and in her place stood a man, and Susan was murmuring words of acknowledgment to Jessica's economical introduction.

David, too, was blond, and his eyes were darkly blue. He was slender and fairly tall; his mouth was fine and sensitive, and there was a look about his temples and around his eyes that was—Susan sought for the word and found it—wistful. He was young and strong and vibrant—the only young thing in the house—but he was not happy. Susan knew that at once. He said:

"How do you do, Miss Dare?"

"Don't go upstairs yet, David," said Jessica. Her voice was less harsh, she watched him avidly. "You ought to rest."

"Not now, Aunt Jessica. I'll see you again, Miss Dare." He walked away. "Aunt Marie all right?" he called from the stairway.

"Perfectly," said Jessica. Her voice was harsh again. "She's reading——"

Afterward Susan tried to remember whether she could actually hear David's steps upon the padded stairs or whether she was only half consciously calculating the time it took to climb the stairs—the time it took, or might have taken to walk along the hall, to enter a room. She was sure that Jessica did not speak. She merely sat there.

Why did Jessica become rigid and harsh again when David spoke of Marie? Why did——

A loud, dreadful crash of sound forever shattered the silence in the house. It fell upon Susan and immersed her and shook the whole house and then receded in waves. Waves that left destruction and intolerable confusion.

Susan realized dimly that she was on her feet and trying to move toward the stairway, and that Jessica's mouth was gray, and that Jessica's hands were clutching her.

"Oh, my God—David——" said Jessica intelligibly, and Susan pushed the woman away from her.

She reached the stairway, Jessica beside her, and at the top of the stairs two figures were locked together and struggling in the upper hall.

"Caroline," screamed Jessica. "What are you doing? Where's Marie—where——"

"Let me go, Caroline!" David was pulling Caroline's thin clutching arms from around him. "Let me go, I tell you. Something terrible has happened. You must——"

Jessica brushed past them and then was at the door of Marie's room.

"*It's Marie!*" she cried harshly. "*Who shot her?*"

Susan was vaguely conscious of Caroline's sobbing breaths and of David's shoulder pressing against her own. Somehow they had all got to that open doorway and were crowding there together.

It *was* Marie.

She sat in the same chair in which she'd been sitting when Susan saw her so short a time ago.

But her head had fallen forward, her whole body crumpled grotesquely into black silk folds.

Jessica was the first to enter the room. Then David. Susan, feeling sick and shaken, followed. Only Caroline remained in the doorway, clinging to the casing with thin hands, her face like chalk and her lips blue.

"She's been shot," said Jessica. "Straight through the heart." Then she looked at David. "Did Caroline kill her, David?"

"*Caroline* kill Marie! Why, Caroline couldn't kill anything!" he cried.

"Then who killed her?" said Jessica. "You realize, don't you, that she's dead?"

Her dark gaze probed deeper and she said in a grating whisper: "Did you kill her, David?"

"No!" cried David. "*No!*"

"She's dead," said Jessica.

Susan said as crisply as she could: "Why don't you call a doctor?"

Jessica's silk rustled, and she turned to give Susan a long cold look. "There's no need to call a doctor. Obviously she's dead."

"The police, then," said Susan softly. "Obviously, too—she's been murdered."

"The police," cried Jessica scornfully. "Turn

over my own cousin—my own nephew—to the police. Never."

"I'll call them," Susan said crisply, and whirled and left them with their dead.

On the silent stairway her knees began to shake again. So this was what the house had been waiting for. Murder! And this was why Caroline had been afraid. What, then, had she known? Where was the revolver that had shot Marie? There was nothing of the kind to be seen in the room.

The air was hot—the house terribly still—and she, Susan Dare, was hunting for a telephone—calling a number—talking quite sensibly on the whole—and all the time it was entirely automatic action on her part. It was automatic, even when she called and found Jim Byrne.

"I'm here," she said. "At the Wrays'. Marie has been murdered——"

"My God!" said Jim and slammed up the receiver.

The house was so hot. Susan sat down weakly on the bottom step and huddled against the newel post and felt extremely ill. If she were really a detective, of course, she would go straight upstairs and wring admissions out of them while they were shaken and confused and before they'd had time to arrange their several defenses. But she wasn't a detective, and she had no wish to be, and all she wanted just then was to escape. Something moved in the shadows under the stairs—moved. Susan flung her hands to her throat to choke back a scream, and the little monkey whirled out, peered at her worriedly, then darted up the window curtain and sat nonchalantly on the heavy wooden rod.

Her coat and hat were upstairs. She couldn't go out into the cold and fog without them—and Jim Byrne was on the way. If she could hold out till he got there——

David was coming down the stairs.

"She says it's all right to call the police," he said in a tight voice.

"I've called them."

He looked down at her and suddenly sat on the bottom step beside her.

"It's been hell," he said quite simply. "But I didn't think of—murder." He stared at nothing, and Susan could not bear the look of horror on his young face.

"I understand," she said, wishing she did understand.

"I didn't," he said. "Until—just lately. I knew—oh, since I was a child I've known I must——"

"Must what?" said Susan gravely.

He flushed quickly and was white again.

"Oh, it's a beastly thing to say. I was the only —child, you know. And I grew up knowing that I dared have no—no favorite—you see? If there'd been more of us—or if the aunts had married and had their own children—but I didn't understand how—how violent—" the word stopped in his throat, and he coughed and went on—"how strongly they felt——"

"Who?"

"Why, Aunt Jessica, of course. And Aunt Marie. And Aunt Caroline."

"Too many aunts," said Susan dryly. "What was it they were violent about?"

"The house. And each other. And—and other things. Oh, I've always known, but it was all—hidden, you know. The surface was—all right."

Susan groped through the fog. The surface was all right, he'd said. But the fog parted for a rather sickening instant and gave her an ugly glimpse of an abyss below.

"Why was Caroline afraid?" said Susan.

"*Caroline?*" he said, staring at her. "*Afraid!*" His blue eyes were brilliant with anxiety and excitement. "See here," he said, "if you think it was Caroline who killed Marie, it wasn't. She couldn't. She'd never have dared. I m-mean—" he was stammering in his excitement—"I mean, Caroline wouldn't hurt a fly. And Caroline wouldn't have opposed Marie about anything. Marie—you don't know what Marie was like."

"Exactly what happened in the upstairs hall?"

"You mean—when the shot——"

"Yes."

"Why, I—I was in my room—no, not quite—I was nearly at the door. And I heard the shot. And it's queer, but I believe—I believe I knew right away that it was a revolver shot. It was as if I had expected——" he checked himself. "But I *hadn't* expected—I—" he stopped; dug his fists desperately into his pockets and was suddenly firm and controlled—"but I hadn't actually expected it, you understand."

"Then when you heard the shot you turned, I suppose, and looked."

"Yes. Yes, I think so. Anyway, there was Caroline in the hall, too. I think she was screaming. We were both running. I thought of Marie—I don't know why. But Caroline clutched at me and held me. She didn't want me to go into Marie's room. She was terrified. And then I think you were there and Jessica. Were you?"

"Yes. And there was no one else in the hall? No one came from Marie's room?"

His face was perplexed, terribly puzzled.

"Nobody."

"Except—Caroline?"

"But I tell you it couldn't have been Caroline."

The doorbell began to ring—shrill sharp peals that stabbed the shadows and the thickness of the house.

"It's the police," thought Susan, catching her breath sharply. The boy beside her had straightened and was staring at the wide old door that must be opened.

Behind them on the padded stairway something rustled. "It's the police" said Jessica harshly. "Let them in."

Susan had not realized that there would be so many of them. Or that they would do so much. Or that an inquiry could last so long. She had not realized either how amazingly thorough they were with their photographs and their fingerprinting and their practised and rapid and incredibly searching investigation. She was a little shocked and more than a little awed, sheerly from witnessing at first hand and with her own eyes what police actually did when there was murder.

Yet her own interview with Lieutenant Mohrn was not difficult. He was brisk, youthful, kind, and Jim Byrne was there to explain her presence. She had been very thankful to see Jim Byrne, who arrived on the heels of the police.

"Tell the police everything you know," he had said.

"But I don't know anything."

And it was Lieutenant Mohrn who, oddly enough, brought Susan into the very center and hub of the whole affair.

But that was later—much later. After endless inquiry, endless search, endless repetitions, endless conferences. Endless waiting in the gloomy dining room with portraits of dead and vanished Wrays staring fixedly down upon policemen. Upon Susan. Upon servants whose alibis had, Jim had informed her, been immediately and completely established.

It was close to one o'clock when Jim came to her again.

"See here," he said. "You look like a ghost. Have you had anything to eat?"

"No," said Susan.

A moment later she was in the kitchen, accepting provender that Jim Byrne brought from the icebox.

"You do manage to get things done," she said. "I thought newspaper men wouldn't even be permitted in the house."

"Oh, the police are all right—they'll give a statement to all of us—treat us right, you know. More cake? And don't forget I'm in on this case. Have you found out yet what Caroline was afraid of?"

"No. I've not had a chance to talk to her. Jim, who did it?"

He smiled mirthlessly.

"You're asking me! They've established, mainly, three things: the servants are clear; there was no one in the house besides Jessica and David and Caroline."

"And me," said Susan with a small shudder. "And—Marie."

"And you," agreed Jim imperturbably. "And Marie. Third, they can't find the gun. Jessica and you alibi each other. That leaves David and Caroline. Well—which of them did it? And why?"

"I don't know," she said. "But, Jim, I'm frightened."

"*Frightened!* With the house full of police? Why?"

"I don't know," said Susan again. "It's nothing I can explain. It's just—a queer kind of menace. Somewhere—somehow—in this house. It's like Marie—only Marie is dead and this is alive. Horribly alive." Susan knew she was incoherent and that Jim was staring at her worriedly, and suddenly the swinging door behind her opened, and Susan's heart leaped to her throat before the policeman spoke.

"The lieutenant wants you both, please," he said.

As they passed through the hall, the clock struck a single note that vibrated long afterward. It had been, then, eight hours and more since she had entered that wide door and been met by Jessica.

Lights were on everywhere now, and there were policemen, and the old-fashioned sliding doors between the hall and the drawing room had been closed, and they shut in the sound of voices.

"In there," said the policeman and drew back one of the doors.

It was entirely silent in the heavily furnished room. Lights were on in the chandelier above and it was eerily, dreadfully bright. The streaks showed in the faded brown velvet curtains at the windows, and the wavery lines in the mantelpiece mirror, and the worn spots in the old Turkish rug. And every gray shadow on Jessica's face was darker, and the fine, sharp lines around Caroline's mouth and her haunted eyes showed terribly clear, and there were two bright scarlet spots in David's cheeks. Lieutenant Mohrn had lost his look of youth and freshness and looked the weary, graying forty that he was. A detective in plain clothes was sitting on the small of his back in one of the slippery plush chairs.

The door slid together again behind them, and still no one spoke, although Jessica turned to look at them. And, oddly, Susan had a feeling that everything in that household had changed.

Yet Jessica had not actually changed; her eyes met Susan's with exactly the same cold, remote command. Then what was it that was different?

Caroline—Susan's eyes went to the thin bent figure, huddled tragically on the edge of her chair. Her fine hair was in wisps about her face; her mouth tremulous.

Why, of course! It was not a change. It was merely that both Jessica and Caroline had become somehow intensified. They were both etched more sharply. The shadows were deeper, the lines blacker.

Lieutenant Mohrn turned to Caroline. "This is the young woman you refer to, isn't it, Miss Caroline?"

Caroline's eyes fluttered to Susan, avoided Jessica, and returned fascinated to Lieutenant Mohrn. "Yes—yes."

David whirled from the window and crossed to stand directly above Caroline.

"Look here, Aunt Caroline, you realize that whatever you tell Miss Dare, she'll be bound to tell the police? It's just the same thing—you know that, don't you?"

"Oh, yes, David. That's what—*he*—said."

Lieutenant Mohrn cleared his throat abruptly and a bit uncomfortably.

"She understands that, Wray. I don't know why she won't tell me. But she won't. And she says she will talk to Miss Dare."

"Caroline," said Jessica, "is a fool." She moved rigidly to look at Caroline, who refused to meet her eyes, and said: "You'll find Caroline's got nothing to tell."

Caroline's eyes went wildly to the floor, to the curtains, to David, and both her hands fluttered to her trembling mouth.

"I'd rather talk to her," she said.

"Caroline," said Jessica, "you are behaving irrationally. You have been like this for days. You brought this—this Susan Dare into the house. You lied to me about her—told me it was a daughter of a school friend. I might have known you had no such intimate friend!" She shot a dark look at Susan and swept back to Caroline. "Now you've told the police that you were afraid and that you telephoned to a perfect stranger——"

"Jim Byrne," fluttered Caroline. "His father and my father——"

"That means nothing," said Jessica harshly.

"Don't interrupt me. And then this young woman comes into our house. Why? Answer me, Caroline. Why?"

"I—was afraid——"

"Of what?"

"I—I—" Caroline stood, motioning frantically with her hands—"I'll tell. I'll tell Miss Dare. She'll know what to do."

"This is the situation, Miss Dare," said Lieutenant Mohrn patiently. "Miss Caroline has admitted that she was alarmed about something and why you are here. She has also admitted that there was an urgent and pressing problem that was causing dissension in the household. But she's—very tired, as you see—a little nervous, perhaps. And she says she is willing to tell, but that she prefers talking to you." He smiled wearily. "At any rate (it's asking a great deal of you), but will you hear what she has to tell? It's—a whim, of course." There was something friendly and kind in the look he gave Caroline. "But we'll humor her. And she understands——"

"I understand," said Caroline with a flash of decision. "But I don't want—anyone but Susan Dare."

"Nonsense, Caroline," said Jessica, "I have a right to hear. So has David."

Caroline's eyes, glancing this way and that to avoid Jessica, actually met Jessica's gaze, and she succumbed at once.

"Yes, Jessica," she said obediently.

"All right, then. Now, we are going outside, Miss Caroline. You can say anything you want to say. And remember we are here only to help." Lieutenant Mohrn paused at the sliding door, and Susan saw a look flash between him and Jim Byrne. She also saw Jim Byrne's hand go to his pocket and the brief little nod he gave the lieutenant.

"Do you mind if I stay in the room but out of earshot, Miss Jessica?" Jim asked.

"No," Jessica agreed grudgingly.

"We'll be just outside," said Lieutenant Mohrn, speaking to Jim. Something in his voice added: "Ready for any kind of trouble." She saw, too, the look in Jim's eyes as he glanced at her and then back to the lieutenant, and all at once she understood the meaning of that look and the meaning of his gesture toward his pocket. He had a revolver there, then. And the lieutenant was promising protection. But that meant that they were going to leave her alone with the Wrays. Alone with three people, one of whom was a murderer.

But she was not entirely alone. Jim Byrne was there, in the far corner, his eyes wary and alert and his smile unperturbed.

"Very well now, Caroline," said Jessica. "Let's hear your precious story."

"It's about the house," began Caroline, looking at Susan as if she dared not permit her glance to swerve. "The police dragged it out of me——"

Jessica laughed harshly and interrupted.

"So that's your important evidence. I can tell it with less foolishness. It is simply that we have had an offer of a considerable sum of money for the purchase of this house. We happen to hold this house—all four of us—with equal interest. Thus it is necessary for us to agree before we can sell or otherwise dispose of the property. That's really all there is to it. Caroline and David wanted to sell. I didn't care."

"But Marie didn't want to sell," cried Caroline. "And Marie was stronger than any of us."

"Miss Caroline," said Susan softly. "Why were you afraid?"

For a dreadful second or two there was utter silence.

Then, as dreadfully, Caroline collapsed into her chair again and put her hands over her mouth and moaned.

But Jessica was ready to speak.

"She had nothing to be afraid of. She's merely nervous—very nervous. I know, Caroline, what you have been doing with every cent of money you could get your silly hands upon. But I intended to do nothing about it."

Caroline had given up her effort to avoid Jessica. She was staring at her like a terrified, panting bird.

"You—know——" she gasped in a thin, high voice.

"Of course, I know. You are completely transparent, Caroline. I know that you were gambling away your inheritance—or at least what you could touch——"

"Gambling!" cried David. "What do you mean?"

"Stocks," said Jessica harshly. "Speculative stocks. It got her like a fever. Caroline has always been susceptible. So you have no money at all left, Caroline? Is that why you were so anxious to sell the house? You surely haven't been fool enough to buy on margin."

Caroline's distraught hands confessed what her trembling lips could not speak.

David was suddenly standing beside her, his hand on her thin shoulder.

"Don't worry, Aunt Carrie," he said. "It'll be all right. You've got enough in trust to take care of you."

Over Caroline's head he looked at Jessica. The look or the tenderness in his voice when he spoke to Caroline seemed to infuriate Jessica, and she arose amid a rustling of silk and stood there tall and rigid, facing him.

"Why don't you offer to take care of her yourself, David?" she said gratingly.

David was white, and his eyes brilliant with pain, but he replied steadily: "You know why, Aunt Jessica. And you know why she gambled, too. We were both trying to make enough money to get away. To get away from this house. To get away from——" He stopped.

"From what, David?" said Jessica.

"From Marie," said David desperately. "And from you."

Jessica did not move. Her face did not change.

There was only a queer luminous flash in her eyes. After a horribly long moment she said:

"I loved you far better than Marie loved you, David. You feared her. I intended to give you money when you came to me. You *had* to come to me. You would have begged me for help—me, Jessica! Why did you or Caroline kill Marie? Was it because she refused to sell the house? I know why she refused. She pretended that it was sentiment; that she, the adopted daughter, was more a Wray than any of us. But it wasn't that, really. She hated us. And we wanted to sell. That is, you and Caroline wanted to sell for your own selfish interests. I—it made no difference to me."

Caroline sobbed and cried jerkily:

"But you did care, Jessica. You wanted the money. You—you love money." There was a strangely incredulous wail in her thin voice. "*Money—money!* Not the things it will buy. Not the freedom it might give you. But money—bonds, mortgages, gold. You love money first, Jessica, and you———"

"*Caroline*," said Jessica in a terrible voice. Caroline babbled and sobbed into silence. "Caroline, you are not responsible. You forget that there are strangers here. That Marie has been murdered. Try to collect yourself. At once. You are making a disgusting exhibition."

All three looked at Susan.

And as suddenly as they had been diverted from each other they were, for a moment, united in their feeling against Susan. She was the intruder, the instrument of the police, placed there by the law for the purpose of discovering evidence.

Their eyes were not pleasant.

Susan smoothed back her hair, and she was acutely aware of the small telegram of warning that ran along her nerves. One of them had murdered. She turned to Caroline.

"Then were you afraid that Marie would discover what you had been doing with your money?" she asked gently.

Caroline blinked and was immediately ready to reply, her momentary feeling against Susan disseminated by the small touch of kindness in Susan's manner.

"No," she said in a confidential way. "That wasn't what I was afraid of."

"Then was there something unusual about the house? Something that troubled you?"

"Oh, yes, yes," said Caroline.

"What was it?" asked Susan, scarcely daring to breathe. If only Jessica would remain silent for another moment.

But Caroline was fluttering again.

"I don't know. I don't know. You see, it was all so queer, Marie holding out against us all, and we all—except Jessica sometimes—obeyed Marie. We've always obeyed Marie. Everything in the house has done that. Even Spider—the—the monkey, you know."

Susan permitted her eyes to flicker toward Jessica. She stood immovable, watching David. Susan could not interpret that dark look, and she did not try. Instead she leaned over to Caroline, took her fluttering, ineffectual hands, and said, still gently: "Tell me exactly why you telephoned to Jim Byrne. What was it that happened in the morning—or maybe the night before—that made you afraid?"

"How did you know?" said Caroline. "It happened that night."

"What was it?" said Susan so softly that it was scarcely more than a whisper.

But Caroline quite suddenly swerved.

"I wasn't afraid of Marie," she said. "But everyone obeyed Marie. Even the house always seemed more Marie's house than—than Jessica's. But I didn't kill Marie."

"Tell me," repeated Susan. "What happened last night that was—queer?"

"Caroline," said Jessica harshly, dragging herself back from some deep brooding gulf "you've said enough."

Susan ignored her and held Caroline's feverishly bright eyes with her own. "*Tell me*——"

"It was—Marie——" gasped Caroline.

"Marie—what did she do?" said Susan.

"She didn't do anything," said Caroline. "It was what she said. No, it wasn't that exactly. It was——"

"If you insist upon talking, Caroline, you might at least try to be intelligible," said Jessica coldly.

Could she get Jessica out of the room? thought Susan; probably not. And it was all too obvious that she was standing by, permitting Caroline to talk only so long as Caroline said nothing that she, Jessica, did not want her to say. Susan said quietly: "Did you hear Marie speak?"

"Yes, that was just it," cried Caroline eagerly. "And it was so very queer. That is, of course we—that is, I—have often thought that Marie must be about the house much more than she pretended to be, in order to know all the things she knew. That is, she always knew everything that happened in the house. It—sometimes it was queer, you know, because it was like—like magic or something. It was quite," said Caroline with an unexpected burst of imagery, "as if she had one of those astral body things, and it walked all around the house while Marie just sat there in her room."

"Astral—body—things," said Jessica deliberately. Caroline crimsoned and Jessica's hands gestured outward as much as to say: "You see for yourself what a state she's in."

The old room was silent again. Susan's heart was pounding, and again those small tocsins of warning were sounding in some subconscious realm. All those forces were silently, invisibly combating—struggling against each other. And somewhere amid them was the truth—quite tangible—altogether real.

"But the astral body," said Caroline suddenly into the silence, "couldn't have talked. And I heard Marie speak. She was in Jessica's room, and the door was closed, and I heard her talking to Jessica. And then—that's what's queer—I went straight on past the door and into Marie's room, and there was Marie sitting there. Isn't it queer?"

"Why were you frightened?"

"Because—because——" Caroline's hands twisted together. "I don't know why. Except that I had a—a feeling."

"Nonsense." Jessica laughed. There was again the luminous flash in her shadowed eyes, and she spoke more rapidly than usual. "You see, Susan Dare, how nonsensical all this is. How utterly fantastic!"

"There was Marie," said Caroline. "She was talking to you."

Jessica's silks rustled, and she walked rigidly and quickly to Caroline and leaned over so that she could grip Caroline's shoulder and force Caroline to meet her eyes. David tried to intervene, and she brushed him away and said hoarsely:

"Caroline, you poor little fool. You thought you'd get this young woman here and try to establish your innocence of the crime. All this talk is sheer nonsense. You are cunning after the way of fools such as you. Tell me this, Caroline ——" She paused long enough to take a great gasp of breath. She was more powerful, more invincible than Susan had seen her. "Tell me. Where was David when the revolver was fired?"

Caroline was shrinking backward. David said quickly: "She'll say anything to protect me. She'll say anything, and you———"

"Be quiet, David. Caroline, answer me."

"He was at the door of his room," said Caroline.

For a long moment Jessica waited. Then with terrible deliberation she relaxed her grip and straightened and looked slowly from one to the other.

"You've as good as confessed, Carrie," she said. "There was no one else. You admit that it was not David. Why did you kill her, Carrie?"

"She didn't kill her!" David was between the two women, his face white and his eyes blazing, "It was you, Jessica. You———"

"*David! Stop!*" The two sharp exclamations were like lashes. "I was here in this room when the shot was fired. I didn't kill Marie. I couldn't have killed her. You know that. Come, Caroline."

She put her gray hand upon Caroline's shoulder. Caroline, as if mesmerized by that touch, arose, and Jessica turned to the doorway No one moved as the two women crossed the room. Jim Byrne glanced at Susan unrevealingly and then, at Jessica's imperious gesture, opened the door. Susan was vaguely aware that there were men in the hall outside, but she was held as if enchanted by the extraordinary scene she was witnessing.

No one moved, and there was no sound save the rustle of Jessica's silks while she led Caroline to the stairway. At the bottom step Jessica turned, and there was suddenly something less harsh in her face; it was for an instant almost kind, and there was a queer sort of tenderness in the pressure of her hand upon Caroline's shrinking shoulder.

But that hand was nevertheless compelling.

"Go upstairs," she said to Caroline, in a voice loud enough so that they all heard. "Go upstairs and do what is necessary. There's enough veronal on my dresser. We'll give you time."

She turned as if to barricade the stairway with her own rigid body and looked slowly and defiantly around her. "I'll *make them* give you time, Carrie. *Go on.*"

There was the complete and utter silence of

sheer horror. And in that silence something small and gray and quick flashed down from the curtain and up the stairs.

"Holy Mother," cried someone. "What was that?"

And David sprang forward.

"You can't do that—you can't do that! Caroline, don't move——" Susan knew that he was thrusting himself between Jessica and Caroline, that there was sudden confusion. But she was mainly aware of something that had clicked in her own mind.

Somehow she got through the confusion in the hall to Lieutenant Mohrn, and Jim Byrne was at her side. Both of them listened to the brief words she said; Lieutentant Mohrn ran rapidly upstairs, and Jim disappeared toward the dining room.

Jim was back first. He pulled Susan to one side.

"You are right," he said. "The cook and the houseman both say that Marie was very strict about the monkey and that the monkey always obeyed her. But what do you mean?"

"I'm not sure, Jim. But I've just told Lieutenant Mohrn that I think there should be a bullet hole somewhere upstairs. It was made by the second bullet. It is in the ceiling, perhaps—or wall. I think it's in Jessica's room."

Lieutenant Mohrn was coming down the stairway. He reached the bottom of the stairs and looked wearily and a bit sadly at the group there. At Caroline crumpled against the wall. At David white and taut. At Jessica, a rigid figure of hatred. Then he sighed and looked at the policeman nearest him and nodded.

"Will you go into the drawing-room, please," he asked Susan. "And you, Jim."

The doors slid together and, still wearily, Lieutenant Mohrn pulled out from his pocket a revolver, a long cord, a piece of cotton, and a small alarm clock.

"They were all there hidden in the newel post at the top of the stairway. The carved top was loose as you remembered it, Miss Dare. And there's two shots gone from the revolver, and there's a bullet hole in the wall of Jessica's bedroom. How did you know it was Jessica, Miss Dare?"

"It was the monkey," said Susan. Her voice

sounded unnatural in her own ears, terribly tired, terribly sad. "It was the monkey all the time. You see, he was sitting there, stealing candy *right beside Marie's chair*. He would have been afraid to do that if he had not known, she was dead. And when Jessica entered the room he fled. When I thought of that, the whole thing fell together: the hot house, obviously to keep Marie's body warm and confuse the time of death; everyone out of the house to permit Jessica to do murder; then this thing you've found——"

"It's simple, of course," said Lieutenant Mohrn. "The cord fastened tight between the alarm lever and the trigger—the bit of cotton to pad the alarm. The clock is set for ten minutes after five. When did she hide it in the newel post?"

"When I went down to telephone the police, I suppose, and David and Caroline were in Marie's room.—I want to go home," said Susan wearily.

"Look here," said Jim Byrne. "This sounds all right, Susan, but, remember, Marie couldn't have been dead then. You heard her talk."

"I had never heard her speak before. And I

heard the flat, dead tone of a person who has been deaf a long time. It was Caroline who actually solved the thing. And Jessica knew it. She knew it and at once tried to fasten the blame upon Caroline—to compel her to commit suicide."

"What did Caroline say?" Lieutenant Mohrn was very patient.

"She said that she'd heard Marie speaking with Jessica in Jessica's room behind a closed door. And that she'd gone straight on past that door to Marie's room and found Marie sitting there. Caroline was confused, frightened, talked of astral bodies. Naturally, we knew that Jessica was—rehearsing—her imitation of Marie's way of speaking."

"Premeditated," said Jim. "Planned to the last detail. And your coming merely gave her the opportunity. You were to provide the alibi, Susan."

Susan shivered.

"That was the trouble. She was sitting directly opposite me when the shot was fired upstairs. Yet she was the only person who hated Marie sufficiently to—murder her. It wasn't money. It was hatred. Growing for years in this horrible house, nourished by jealousy over David, brought to a climax that was inevitable," Susan smoothed her hair. "Please may I go?"

"Then Marie was dead when you entered the house?"

"Yes. Propped up by pillows. I—I saw the whole thing, you know. Saw Jessica approach her and talk, heard the reply—and how was I to know it was Jessica speaking and not Marie? Then Jessica bent and did something to her cushions, pulled them away, I suppose, so the body was no longer erect. And she turned at once and was between me and Marie all the way to the door so I could not see Marie, then, at all. (I couldn't see Marie very well at any time, because she was in the shadow.) And when David and Caroline came upstairs, Jessica warned both of them that Marie was reading. I suppose she knew that they were only too glad to be relieved of the necessity to speak to Marie." Susan shivered again and smoothed back her hair and felt dreadfully that she might cry. "It's a t-terrible house," she said indecisively, and Jim Byrne said hurriedly:

"She can go now, can't she? I've got a car out here. She doesn't have to see them again."

The air was cold and fresh and the sky very black before dawn, and the pavements glistened. They swerved onto the Drive and stopped for a red light, and Jim turned to her as they waited. Through the dusk in the car she could feel his scrutiny.

"I didn't expect anything like this," he said gravely. "Will you forgive me?"

"Next time," said Susan in a small clear voice, "I'll not get scared."

"Next time!" said Jim derisively. "There won't be a next time! I was the one that was scared. I had my finger on the trigger of a revolver all the time you were talking to them. No, indeedy, there won't be a next time. Not for you, my girl."

"Oh, all right," said Susan agreeably.

### Easter Devil

SUSAN DARE SIPPED HER COFFEE and quietly contemplated devils. Outside, rain beat down upon cold, dark streets, but inside the drawn curtains of Susan's small library it was warm, with a fire cheerful in the grate, and the dog lazy upon the rug, and cigarettes and an old book beside the deepest armchair. An armchair which Susan just then decorated, for she had dressed for her dinner *à seul* in soft trailing crimson. Too bad, thought Susan regretfully, that her best moments were so often wasted: a seductive crimson gown, and no one to see it. She smashed her cigarette sadly and returned to her book.

Devils and devil-possessed souls! Of course there were no such things, but it was curious how real the old writers made both. Susan, who was a successful young writer of thrilling mystery novels, was storing up this knowledge for future use.

Then the doorbell rang. The dog barked and scrambled to his feet and bounced into the hall, and Susan followed.

Two men, beaten and wet with rain, were waiting, and one of them was Jim Byrne, with a package under his arm.

"Company?" asked Jim tersely, looking at the dress.

"No. I was alone——"

"You remember Lieutenant Mohrn?"

Of course she did! It was her volunteer work with him on a recent Chicago crime that had led the police force to regard her as a valuable consultant.

"How do you do?" said Lieutenant Mohrn. "I hope you don't mind our coming. You see, there's something——"

"Something queer," said Jim. "In point of fact, it's——"

"Murder," said Lieutenant Mohrn.

"Oh," said Susan. Her own small warm house—and these two men with sober faces looking at her. She smoothed back her hair. "Oh," she said again.

Jim pushed the package toward her.

"I got size thirty-six," he said. "Is that right?—I mean, that's what we want you to wear."

That was actually Susan's introduction to the

case of the Easter Devil. Fifteen minutes later she was getting out of the glamorous crimson gown and into a brown tweed suit with a warm topcoat, and tossing a few things into a bag—the few things included the contents of the package, which proved to be several nurse's uniforms, complete with caps, and a small kit of tools which were new and shiny.

"Do you know anything about nursing?" Jim Byrne had asked.

"Nothing," said Susan. "But I've had appendicitis."

"Oh," said Jim, relieved. "Then you can—oh, take a pulse, make a show of nursing. She's not sick, you know. If she were, we could not do this."

"I can shake a thermometer without dropping it," said Susan. "If the doctor will help——"

"Oh, he'll help all right," said Lieutenant Mohrn somewhat grimly. "We have his consent and approval."

She pulled a small brown hat over her hair and then remembered to change gold slippers to brown oxfords.

In the hall Jim was waiting.

"Mohrn had to go," he said. "I'll take you out. Glenn Ash is about an hour's run from town."

"All right," said Susan. She scribbled a note to Huldah and spoke soberly to the dog, who liked to have things explained to him.

"I'm going to a house in Glenn Ash," she said gravely. "Be a good dog. And don't chase the neighbor's cat."

He pushed a cold nose against her hand. He didn't want her to go, and he thought the matter of Petruchkin the cat might better have been ignored. Then the front door closed and he heard presently two doors bang and a car drive away. He returned to the library. But he was gradually aware that the peace and snugness were gone. He felt gloomily that it would have been very much better if the woman had stayed at home.

And the woman, riding along a rainswept road, rather agreed with him. She peered through the rain-shot light lanes ahead and reviewed in her mind the few facts that she knew. And they were brief enough.

At the home of one Gladstone Denisty in Glenn Ash a servant had been murdered. Had been shot in the back and found (where he'd fallen) in a ravine near the house. There was no weapon found, and anyway he couldn't have shot himself. There were no signs of attempted burglary. There were, indeed, no clues. He was a quiet, well-behaved man and an efficient servant and had been with the Denisty family for some time; so far as could be discovered, his life held no secrets.

Yet that morning he had been found in the ravine, murdered.

The household consisted of Gladstone Denisty and his wife; his mother and brother, and two remaining servants.

"It's Mrs. Gladstone Denisty—her first name is Felicia—whom we want you to nurse," Lieutenant Mohrn had said. "There's more to the thing than meets the eye. You see, the only lead we have leads to the Denisty home; this man was killed by a bullet of the same caliber as that of a revolver which is known to have been in the Denisty house—property of nobody in particular—and which has disappeared within the last week. But that's all we know. And we thought if we could get you inside the house—just to watch things, you know. There's no possible danger to you."

"There's always danger," said Jim brusquely, "where there's murder."

"If Miss Dare thinks there's danger, she's to leave," said Lieutenant Mohrn wearily. "All I want her to do is get a—line on things."

And Jim, somehow grudgingly, had said nothing; still said nothing.

It was a long ride to Glenn Ash, and that night a difficult one, owing to the rain and wind. But they did finally turn off the winding side road into a driveway and stop.

Susan could barely see the great dark bulk of the house looming above with only a light or two showing.

Then Jim's hand was guiding her up some brick steps and across a wide veranda. He put his mouth to her ear: "If anything happens that you don't like, leave. At once." And Susan whispered, "I will," and Jim was gone, and the wide door was opening, and a very pretty maid was taking her bag and leading her swiftly upstairs. The household had retired, said the maid, and Mrs. Denisty would see her in the morning.

"You mean Mrs. Gladstone Denisty?" asked Susan.

"Oh, no, ma'am. *Mrs.* Denisty," said the

maid. "Is there anything——? Thank you. Good-night, ma'am."

Susan, after a thoughtful moment, locked her door and presently went to bed and listened to the rain against the windowpanes and wished she could sleep. However, she must have fallen asleep, for she awakened suddenly and in fright. It had stopped raining. And somewhere there had been a sound.

There had been a sound, but it was no more. She only knew that it had waked her and that she was ridiculously terrified. And then all at once her heart stopped its absurd pounding and was perfectly still. For something—out there in the long and empty hall—had brushed against her bedroom door!

She couldn't, either then or later, have persuaded herself to go to that door and open it and look into the hall. And anyway, as the moments dragged on, she was convinced that whoever or whatever had brushed against her door was gone. But she sat, huddled under blankets, stonily wide awake until slow gray dawn began to crawl into the room. Then she fell again into sleep, only to be waked this time by the maid, carrying a breakfast tray and looking what she thought of trained nurses who slept late. Mrs. Denisty, she informed Susan, wished to see her.

Not, thought Susan, getting into the unaccustomed uniform, an auspicious beginning. And she was shocked to discover that she looked incredibly young and more than a little flip in the crisply tailored white dress and white cap. She took her horn-rimmed spectacles, which improved things very little, and her thermometer, and went downstairs, endeavoring to look stern enough to offset the unfortunate effect of the cap.

But on the wide landing of the stairs she realized that the thick, white-haired woman in the hall below was interested only in the tongue-lashing she was giving two maids. They were careless, they were lying, they had broken it— all of it. She looked up just then and saw Susan and became at once bland.

"Good-morning, Miss Dare," she said. "Will you come down?" She dismissed the servants and met Susan at the foot of the stairs. "We'll go into this drawing room," she said. She wore a creamy white wool dress with blue beads and a blue handkerchief and did not ask Susan to sit down.

"The household is a little upset just now," she

said. "There was an unfortunate occurrence here, night before last. Yes—unfortunate. And then yesterday or last night the maid or cook or somebody managed to break some Venetian glass—quite a lot of it—that my daughter-in-law was much attached to. Neither of them will admit it. However, about my daughter-in-law, Mrs. Gladstone Denisty, whom you are here to care for: I only wished to tell you, Miss Dare, that her nerves are bad, and the main thing, I believe, is merely to humor her. And if there is anything you wish to know, or if any—problem—arises, come to me. Do you understand?"

Susan wondered what was wrong with the room and said she understood.

"Very well," said Mrs. Denisty, rising. "That is all."

But that was not all. For there was a whirlwind of steps, and a voice sobbing broken phrases swept through the door, and a woman ran into the room clutching in both hands something bright and crimson. A queer little chill that she could never account for crept over Susan as she realized that the woman clutched, actually, broken pieces of glass.

"Did you see, Mother Denisty?" sobbed the

woman. "It's all over the floor. How much more—how much more——"

"Felicia!" cried Mrs. Denisty sternly. "Hush—yes, I know. It was an accident."

"An accident! But you know—you know——"

"The nurse is here—Miss Dare."

The young woman whirled. She was—or had been—of extraordinary beauty. Slender and tall, with fine, fair hair and great, brilliant gray eyes. But the eyes were hollow and the lids swollen and pink, and her mouth pale and uncertain.

"But I don't need a nurse."

"Just for a few days," said Mrs. Denisty firmly. "The doctor advised it."

The great gray eyes met Susan's fixedly—too fixedly, indeed, for the look was actually an unwavering stare. Was there something, then, beyond Susan—near Susan—that she did not wish to see?

"*Oh*," said Felicia Denisty with a thin sharp gasp and looked at her hand, and Susan ran forward. On the slender white hand was a brighter, thicker crimson than the Venetian glass which was just then and quite slowly relinquished.

"You've cut your hand," said Susan inadequately. Felicia had turned to the older woman, who was unmoved.

"See," she said, extending her bleeding hand. "Just to be in the room with it——"

Mrs. Denisty moved forward then.

"Will you go upstairs with Mrs. Gladstone, Miss Dare," she said firmly, "and dress her hand."

Upstairs Susan blessed a brief course of Red Cross lectures which during school days she had loathed, and made a fairly workmanlike job of bandaging the wound.

But it was not so easy to spend the long hours of the slow gray day with Felicia Denisty, for she had fallen into a brooding silence, sat and stared either at her bandaged hand or out the window upon a dreary balcony, and said practically nothing.

The afternoon passed much as the morning, except that with the approach of dusk the wind rose a bit and rattled shutters, and Felicia grew restless and turned on every available light in her room.

"Dinner," she said to Susan, "is at seven-thirty." She looked fully at Susan, as if for the first time. "You've been inside all day, Miss

Dare. I didn't think—would you like to take a walk before dinner?"

Susan said she would, and hoped she wasn't too eager.

But at the end of half an hour's walk through rapidly increasing gray dusk she was still no wiser than she had been, except that she had a clearer notion of the general plan of the house— built like a wide-flung T with tall white pillars running up to the second-story roof of the wide double porch, which extended across the front of the house—and of the grounds.

On two sides of the house was a placid brown lawn, stretching downward to roadway and to rolling meadows. But on the south lay the ravine, an abrupt, irregular gash, masked now and made mysterious by dripping shrubbery. Beyond it appeared the roof of a house, and at the deepest point of the ravine it was crossed by a small wooden bridge which lost itself in the trees at the farther end. It must lead, thought Susan, to the house, but she did not explore it, although she looked long at the spot where (as revealed by a discreet inquiry of the pretty housemaid) the butler had been murdered.

It was perhaps ten feet from the entrance to

the small wooden bridge and just behind a large clump of sumach. It was not in view from the windows of the Denisty house.

Susan, made oddly uneasy by the fog-enshrouded shadows of the trees, made her way back.

Once inside she turned at once to the drawing room. It was dark, and she fumbled for the light and found it. The room was exactly as she remembered it from the morning; a large room of spaces and many windows and massive furniture. Not somehow a pleasant room. It was too still, perhaps, too chilly, too—she turned suddenly as if someone had spoken her name and saw the Easter image.

And she realized what was wrong with the room.

It stood there beside the fireplace—a black, narrow image of a man—a terribly emaciated man, with protruding ribs and a queer, painted face, roughly carved. It was perhaps two feet tall and there were white marks on it that looked like, but were not chalk. Its emaciation and its protruding ribs suggested that it was a remnant of that strangely vanished race from mysterious, somber Easter Island. When you looked at it analytically, that was all there was to see.

But it was singularly difficult to look at it analytically. And that was because of the curiously repellent look in its face; the air of strange and secret sentience that somehow managed to surround the small figure. There was a hint of something decadent, something faintly macabre, something incredibly and hideously wise. It was intangible: it was not sensible. But, nevertheless, it was there.

Yet, Susan told herself sternly, the image itself was merely a piece of wood.

A carved piece of wood from Easter Island: a souvenir, probably, of a journey there. It had no connection with the murder of a butler, with the shattered fine fragments of Venetian glass.

Susan turned suddenly and left the drawing room. But when in the hall the door behind her opened. Susan all but screamed before she saw the man who had entered. He flung off hat and coat and reached for a stack of letters on the hall table and then finally looked at her and said: "Oh, hullo. You must be the nurse. Miss——"

"Dare," said Susan. He was thick, white-haired, brusque, with a blunt nose and bright, hard blue eyes. He wasn't over forty-five, and he must be a Denisty.

"Dare," said he. "Nice name. Well, take care of my wife." His blue eyes shot a quick glance up the stairway, and he bent and kissed at Susan; turned, humming, toward the library, and vanished.

Kissed at her; for what she felt would have been a rather expert kiss had been pretty well deflected by some quick action on her part.

Well, that was Gladstone.

And Marlowe Denisty, the brother, who turned up at dinner, was a handsome Byronic-looking youth who talked enthusiastically of practically everything.

It was Marlowe who later, in the drawing room, spoke of the Easter image.

He had brought it, he told Susan expansively, from Easter Island himself. It was a present to Gladstone.

"An akuaku," said Susan absently.

"A *what?*" said Gladstone, turning sharply to look at her.

Susan wished she had not spoken, and Marlowe flashed her a glance of bright approval.

"An akuaku," he said. "An evil god. You remember, Glad, I told you all about it when I brought the thing home. These wooden figures, or moai miro, were made first, so far as can be discovered, by Tuukoihu, who ruled the island following Hotu Matua. These small figures with protruding ribs were thought to be reminders of the imminence of death, threats of——"

"Thank you, I can read the encyclopedia myself," said Gladstone Denisty sharply. "And anyway, it's all nonsense. A piece of carved wood with white painting on it can't possibly have any sort of significance."

"It *can* have," cried Felicia with sudden unexpected violence. "It *does* have!"

Mrs. Denisty, with a glance at Gladstone, interrupted. "Felicia, dear child," she cried in a deprecating way. "How can you be so absurd!"

"Hush!" Felicia's voice was all at once taut; her eyes were wide and dark, and she flung out her hand toward the image. "Don't you realize that it hears you? Don't you realize what it has brought into this house? Misfortune—suffering —murder——"

"*Felicia!*" The interruption was loud and covered anything Felicia might have continued to say, and Mrs. Denisty went on swiftly. "You are hysterical, my dear, and not quite yourself. As to misfortune, we have lost no more than other people and are still very comfortable. And your illness couldn't possibly have been induced by a wooden image——"

"An evil god—an evil influence," muttered Felicia, staring at the image.

Mrs. Denisty swept on, though her mouth was tight.

"And William's death, which I suppose you are referring to, was the result of his discovering an attempt to burglarize the house. It is dreadful, of course. But it had no possible connection with this—this piece of wood."

Felicia was trembling. Susan put a hand upon her arm but could not stay the uneven torrent of words.

"What of the things that have happened to me?—Why, even my kitten died. Flowers die if I touch them. Something happens to everything that is mine. Why—just last night—the glass——" She was sobbing. "William—he was kind to me—he——"

Gladstone intervened.

"Take her upstairs, Miss Dare," he said

quietly. "See if you can quiet her. She has some capsules the doctor gave her—try to calm yourself, Felicia."

"Oh, I'll go. I'll go."

She sobbed weakly. But she said no more, and once in her room upstairs took the sedative and afterwards lay quiet, staring at the ceiling with great tragic eyes.

"Your illness," said Susan gently. "The doctor didn't tell me——"

Felicia did not look at her.

"Nerves, he says. That's all any of them say. But I was all right until he brought the image home. About a year ago." The sedative was beginning to take effect, and she spoke calmly. "It is the image, you see, Miss Dare. It hates me. I feel it. I know it. And—I heard the story—of a woman in Tahiti, an Englishwoman who had one, and it hated her, and it brought evil and suffering and misfortune, and finally—death."

She spoke the last word in a whisper.

"Did Marlowe tell you of it?"

"Yes. He told us. We thought nothing of it—then. Mother Denisty says it is wrong of me to fear it. She's religious, you know."

"She holds very firmly to the church?"

"Oh, yes. Except in the modern trend. That is—divorce, you know. She is very much against divorce." Owing perhaps to the capsule, Felicia was beginning to talk in a rambling way. "She says my feeling about the image is superstition."

"How was William kind to you?" asked Susan.

"Oh, in so many little ways. I think he liked me. It was he who told me about the flowers. Of course, I didn't believe him. I know why they died. But he told me that, so I would feel better." She was becoming drowsy, and her words were soft and slow.

Susan felt and stifled with rather shocking ease a scruple against further questions and said: "What did he tell you?"

"Oh—something about acid in the water. I don't know—it couldn't have been true. Flowers died because they were mine. And I don't want to study French any more."

"*French*," said Susan. "*French!*"

Felicia's drooping eyelids flared open. She stared hazily but intently at Susan and suddenly lifted herself on one elbow and leaned toward her and whispered hoarsely: "It's Dorothy. She knows about the image. I can see it in her eyes. In her eyes." She dropped back upon the pillow, repeated "In her eyes—in her eyes," and then quite suddenly was heavily asleep.

After a long time Susan tiptoed away.

But at midnight she was still broadly awake, strongly aware, as one is at night, of the house about her and all that it held—including the thing that brooded over a downstairs room.

Only a piece of wood.

And what possible connection was there between a piece of wood, some shattered fine glass, and a murdered butler? French lessons and dead flowers and an acid? A kitten—dead, also. An image that represented the imminence of death. A hysterical woman—talking of death.

That night, if anyone brushed against her door, Susan did not know it, for she fell at length into an uneasy sleep.

Her second day in the Denisty household was in many ways a replica of the first, except that nothing at all happened.

Once during the morning she heard Mrs. Denisty telephoning to someone she called Dorothy and saying that Felicia would not be able to do

French that morning, which left Susan little wiser than she had been. And once she herself was called to the telephone for what proved to be an extremely guarded conversation with Jim Byrne. She succeeded only in reassuring him as to her own personal safety, told him carefully that she did not know how long the "case" would last, and hung up.

That night, too, was quiet. But the next day things happened.

In the first place, "Dorothy" came to call. Susan, just entering Felicia's room with the morning paper, heard her voice on the stairs.

"Is Mrs. Gladstone in her room?"

"Yes, Mrs. Laasch," replied the housemaid's voice.

"So I thought. No, no—I know the way. Mrs. Gladstone won't mind."

Susan waited. In another moment the owner of the voice came along the hall, glanced at Susan, and preceded her into Felicia's room with the ease of very old and intimate acquaintance.

"Oh, good-morning, Dorothy," said Felicia.

So this was Dorothy. Dorothy Laasch. Susan gave Felicia the paper and at Felicia's gesture sat down near her.

"Mother Denisty tells me there'll be no more French until you are feeling better," Dorothy was saying. She was a handsome woman in perhaps her middle thirties; a blonde with short hair, vivacious if rather large features, and light, swift eyes. She wore a green wool suit, no hat, and suède pumps. Felicia murmured something and Dorothy went on:

"Since Mother Denisty says so, I suppose that settles it. You ought to rouse yourself, Felicia. You let that woman rule you. Just because she controls the purse strings——"

"Dorothy," said Felicia in a remonstrating way.

Dorothy shot a quick glance toward the door into the hall.

"She's outdoors. I met her down by the bridge."

"But——" said Felicia.

"Oh, you mean the nurse." Dorothy looked at Susan and laughed. "Nurses neither hear nor care, do they, Miss——"

"Dare," said Felicia. She turned briefly to Susan. "This is Mrs. Laasch. I thought you'd met. Let's put off the French lessons for a couple of weeks, Dorothy."

"Nonsense," said Dorothy vigorously. "You'll be all right in a day or two. How's Mother Denisty taking this business of William's death?"

"I—don't know," faltered Felicia.

"No, I don't suppose you do know," said Dorothy with something like exasperation. "Really, Felicia, you can't see anything. Have the police done anything?"

"About William, you mean? Nothing more. At least, nothing that I know of."

Dorothy patted Felicia's hand briskly.

"Then why do you worry? Mother Denisty can't live forever. And think of the insurance she——"

"Mother Denisty is very kind to me," said Felicia. Her hands were trembling.

"Kind," said Dorothy. She laughed abruptly. "You are all afraid of her. Every one of——"

"Ah, there you are, Dorothy," said Mrs. Denisty's bland voice from the doorway. Dorothy turned quickly, Felicia bent closer over her knitting, and Susan felt quite suddenly as if something had shifted and moved under her feet. Like quicksand, she thought, only it was nothing so perceptible.

"I hope you've cheered up Felicia," said Mrs.

Denisty. Her eyes were as blank and cold as two blue beads, but her voice was pleasant. If she had heard Dorothy's words, she gave no indication of it.

"I've tried to," said Dorothy. She rose. "I must run now. Good-bye, Felicia. Good-bye, Miss Dare. Good-bye, Mother Denisty."

She kissed Felicia's white face; she kissed Mrs. Denisty. But Susan rose and walked downstairs and out the wide front door with Dorothy, who accepted her company with the breezy manner that seemed characteristic of her.

"Poor Felicia," said Dorothy. "Do walk along to the bridge with me, Miss Dare. The path goes this way. I live just across the ravine, you know. I should be so alone but for Felicia. I'm a widow, you know. Tell me, just how *is* Felicia?"

"She seems not much changed," said Susan.

"That's what I feared. It seems so queer and useless for her to brood over William. I can't imagine——" She checked herself abruptly and then continued in the same rapid way: "I don't believe any of them realize the state Felicia is in. And Miss Dare—I am afraid for her."

"Afraid! Of whom?"

Dorothy paused before she said, very slowly:

"I'm afraid Felicia has Felicia to fear more than anyone else."

Suicide! Brooding over William. Was that what Dorothy meant? At their right was the patch of brown, dripping sumach. Susan said: "That's where the man was murdered, isn't it?"

"About there, I believe," said Dorothy. She met Susan's eyes for a long moment. "Take care of Felicia—watch her, Miss Dare. Goodbye."

Her heels tapped the wooden floor of the bridge. Susan watched, thinking of her last words, until Dorothy's blonde head vanished around the curve in the path beyond the bridge. Then Susan turned. As she did so something about the floor of the bridge caught her eye, and she bent to look.

Presently she rose and very thoughtfully went back to the house. But it was exactly then that terror clutched at Susan and would not be shaken off.

Yet, at the moment, there was nothing at all that she could do. Nothing but wait and listen and look.

It made it no easier when, that dreary afternoon, Felicia talked of death. Talked absently, queerly, knitting on a yellow afghan. What did Susan think it would be—did she think it would be difficult—would one regret at the last—when it was too late—would one——

"Has anyone talked to you—of death?" asked Susan sharply.

"N-no," said Felicia. "That is, Dorothy and I have talked of it. Some. And Marlowe always likes to discuss such things."

"But that is wrong," said Susan abruptly. "You are sad and depressed."

"Perhaps," said Felicia agreeably. She knitted a long row before she said:

"Dear Glad—he is so good to me. He would, really, give me anything I want. Why, he would even give me a divorce if I asked for it: he has often said so. Not that I want a divorce. It only shows that he would put my wishes, even about that, ahead of Mother Denisty's."

"Then why," said Susan very gently, "does he keep the—Easter image?"

Felicia flinched visibly, but replied:

"Why, you see, Miss Dare, he—he believes in its power. And he keeps it because he says it would be very weak to give in to his—feeling about it."

"But he talks as if——" began Susan irrepressibly and checked herself.

"Oh, yes," said Felicia. "But that's only because he doesn't like to admit it to other people."

It was that night that the thing happened in the drawing room. And that was the matter of the yellow afghan.

While they were at dinner, somehow, some time, under the very eyes of the Easter image, the knitting was unraveled.

They found it when they entered the chill and quiet drawing room immediately after dinner. It lay in an untidy heap of crinkly yellow yarn, half on the chair where Felicia had left it, half on the floor.

Felicia saw it first and screamed.

And even Mother Denisty looked gray when she saw the heap of yarn. But she turned at once commandingly to Susan and told her to take Felicia upstairs.

Gladstone took Felicia's arm, and Susan followed, and somehow they got her out of the room. As they passed the still, black Easter image Felicia shuddered.

Upstairs, however, she managed to reply to Gladstone's inquiries.

Yes, she said, she had left the knitting there on the chair just before dinner.

"You are sure, Felicia?"

"Why, of course. I knew we would come into the drawing room for coffee and I—I wanted to have my knitting there. It—keeps me from looking at the image——"

"Nonsense, Felicia. The image won't hurt you."

Felicia wrung her hands.

"Glad, don't keep up this pretense. You know you are afraid of it, too. And Miss Dare knows——"

"Miss Dare——" He turned, his eyes blue and cold and exactly like his mother's, plunged into Susan's eyes and Felicia cried:

"So there's no need to pretend because she is here."

"My wife," said Gladstone to Susan, "seems to be a bit hysterical——"

"Oh, no, no," moaned Felicia. "Don't you see? Listen to me, Glad." She was leaning forward, two scarlet spots in her cheeks and her great eyes blazing. "I left the knitting there in the chair. I was the last one in the dining room—do you remember?"

"Y-yes," said Gladstone unwillingly.

"No one left the table. No one was in the drawing room. And when I returned, it was completely raveled out. Oh, it isn't the knitting that matters: I don't care about that. But it's the—the cruelty. The——" she paused searching for the word, wringing her hands again. Finally it came: "The persecution," said Felicia Denisty.

"Nonsense," said Gladstone heavily. "You are making too much of an absurdly trivial thing. Now, Felicia, do be sensible. Take one of your capsules and go to sleep. The image simply couldn't have pulled your knitting loose—if that's what you mean."

"The image," said Felicia slowly, "couldn't have killed William, either. But William is dead."

"Don't be morbid, Felicia," said Gladstone. He paused with his hand on the door-knob. "Miss Dare, will you help me a moment, please?"

It was, of course, an absurdly transparent excuse. Felicia said nothing and Susan followed Gladstone into the hall. He closed the door.

"Did my wife unravel the knitting herself, Miss Dare?" he said directly.

"I don't know." His hard blue eyes, so strangely like his mother's, were plumbing her own eyes, seeking for any thought that lay behind them.

"She seems to have been talking to you a great deal," he said, slowly.

"No," said Susan quietly, "not a great deal."

He waited for her to say more. But Susan waited, too.

"I hope," he said at length, "that you realize to what her talk is due."

Susan smoothed back her hair.

"Yes," she said truthfully. "I believe I do."

He stared at her again, then suddenly turned away.

"That's good," he said. "Good-night, Miss Dare."

He went down the stairs at once. In a moment, Susan heard the heavy outside door close. He had not, then, joined his mother and Marlowe, whose voices, steadily and blandly talking, were coming from the drawing room. The room where the Easter image brooded and waited. She returned to Felicia.

"I took two capsules," said Felicia wearily. "You needn't stay, Miss Dare. I'll be asleep in no time."

Two capsules. Susan resolved to talk to the doctor the next day, did what she could for Felicia, and left. This time she met Marlowe, his arms full of yellow wool.

"Oh, hello there, Miss Dare," he said. "I was just looking for you. What shall we do with this? Mother is frightfully upset about it. Glad is the apple of her eye, you know. It's never been exactly a happy marriage—you've probably guessed it. Poor mother. And now Felicia's got this queer notion about the Easter image."

"How did she get the notion?" said Susan. "I mean—has it been long?"

"M-m—a few months. Seems to have got worse since these unlucky things have been happening. Just accidents, of course. But it is a bit queer. Isn't it?"

"Very," said Susan. "Tell me, is she interested in the French lessons?"

"With Dorothy, you mean? Oh, I don't know. She goes regularly, nine o'clock every morning. Mother sees to that. But I don't know that she likes it much. Funny thing, psychology, isn't it? I suppose you see a lot of queer things in your profession, don't you?"

"Well," said Susan guardedly, "yes and no. Good-night. Oh, I don't think it would be a good thing to give the yarn to her just now. Anyway, she's asleep."

He turned toward the stairway, his arms still full of yellow yarn.

In her room, Susan locked the door as she had done carefully every night in the silent haunted house. Haunted by a wooden image.

And then, vehemently, she rejected the thought. It was no wooden image that menaced that house and those within it. It was something far stronger.

And yet she was shaken in spite of herself by the incident of the knitting. After all, *had* Felicia herself unraveled it? The family were all at the table and no one left it even momentarily. And the pretty housemaid who was, since William's death, acting as waitress, had been busily occupied and also, naturally, the cook.

But Susan was dealing only with intangibles. There was still no definite, material clue.

She turned, smoothed back her hair, and sat down at the writing desk. And set herself to reducing intangibles to tangibles.

It was after midnight when she leaned back and looked at what she had written.

A conclusion was there, of course, implicit in those facts. But she needed one link. And, even with that one link, she had no proof. Susan turned off the light and opened the window and stood there for a moment, looking out into the starless, quiet night.

Through the darkness and quiet a small dull sound came, beating with rhythmic little thuds upon her ears. And quite suddenly it was as if a small far-away tom-tom was beating out its dark and secret message.

Easter Island and a devil.

"This," said Susan firmly to herself, "is fantastic. The sound is made by footsteps on the wooden bridge."

She listened, and faintly the footsteps came nearer. She could see nothing through the soft damp blackness. But suddenly, not far below her window, the footsteps ceased. Whoever was on the bridge then had now reached the path.

There was no way to know who had passed.

Yet quite suddenly Susan knew as surely as if she had seen.

And with the knowledge came the strangest feeling of urgency. For she knew, with a blinding flash of light, what those footsteps on the bridge meant.

She snatched a dark silk dressing gown and flung it around her shoulders, unlocked her door and fled down the hall. She waited in the dusk above the stair railing, until the door below opened and she caught a glimpse of the person who entered. It was as she expected, and she turned and was at Felicia's door by the time steps began to ascend the stairs.

If Felica's door were locked! But it was not. She opened it and slipped inside and leaned against it, her heart pounding as if she'd been racing. Felicia was sleeping quietly and peacefully.

Now what to do? If there were only time—time to plan, time to make arrangements. But there was not.

And she had no proof.

And the feeling of urgency was stronger.

Felicia lay so sunk in sleep that only her heavy drugged breathing told Susan that she was alive.

At the bedside table was a telephone—a delicate gold and ivory thing—resting on a cradle.

Did she dare use it?

She must take the risk. She would need help.

She went to the telephone, lifted it, and called a number very softly into the ivory mouthpiece, and waited.

"Hello—hello——" It was Jim Bryne's voice and sounded sleepy and far away.

"Jim—Jim, this is Susan."

"Susan—do you want me?"

"Yes." Did she imagine it or did the floor creak very softly just below the door? If anyone were out there, if her voice, not Felicia's, were heard——

"Susan—what are you doing? *Susan*——"

Even at a distance the vibration from the telephone might be heard.

"Susan!" cried Jim and very softly Susan replaced the telephone on its cradle. Suddenly his voice was gone. And he was miles and miles away.

The floor under the door did not creak again. If she could only have told Jim what to do, what she was trying to do, where to wait until she signaled. Well, the thing now was to get Felicia out of danger.

She turned to the bed.

It was terrifically difficult to rouse Felicia. Susan was exhausted and trembling by the time she had managed to half carry and half push Felicia into the small dressing room. A chaise-longue was there, and when Felicia's slack, inert figure collapsed upon it gracelessly, she fell again into the horribly heavy slumber from which she had never fully aroused. And all the time there had been that dreadful necessity for haste.

Susan, panting from the sheer physical strain, very softly closed the door of the dressing room.

Then, with the utmost caution, she turned the shade of the light so that it would not fall directly upon the door into the hall and yet so that anyone entering the room would be obliged to cross that narrow band of light.

Then, because she was shaking from cold and nerves and the strain of the past few moments, she took Felicia's place on the bed. And waited.

And in the waiting, as always happens, she became uncertain. All the other possibilities crowded into her mind. She was mistaken. There was no proof. This attempt to trap the murderer would fail. She was wrong in thinking that the attack would be made that night.

She knew that Jim Byrne, and probably Lieutenant Mohrn and a number of extremely active and husky policemen, were at that very moment speeding along the road to Glenn Ash.

The thought of it was inexpressibly comforting. But it was also fraught with dangerous possibilities. They might easily arrive too soon. They couldn't arrive too late, she thought, as, once she had proof, that was enough.

But there were so many ways the thing could go wrong, thought Susan rather desperately as the minutes ticked away on the little French clock on the mantel. And her own rapidly conceived plan was so weak, so full of loopholes, so dependent upon chance. Or was it?

After all, it had been intuitional, swift, certain. And intuition with her, Susan reminded herself firmly, was actually a matter of subconscious reasoning. And subconscious reasoning, she went on still firmly, was far better than conscious, rule-of-thumb reasoning. And anyway, the rule-of-thumb reasoning was clear too.

The attack upon Felicia must come. It had already been prepared and ready once, but then William, poor William, had come into it and interfered and had had to be murdered.

She was in the deep shadow, there on Felicia's bed. But the door into the hall was in deep shadow, too. Would she hear it when it opened?

How long was it since she had telephoned to Jim? Where was he now? What would he do when he arrived?

She became more and more convinced that the police would arrive too soon.

Yet, unless she was entirely mistaken, the attack must come soon. Although planned perhaps for months, that night it would be in one way an impulsive act.

She did not shift her eyes from the door. It was so quiet in the house—so terribly quiet and so cold. It was as if the Easter image downstairs had extended the realm of his possession. So cold——

It was then that Susan realized that the cold was coming from the window and that it was being opened, moving almost silently inward. Her eyes had jerked that way, and her heart gave a great leap of terror, but otherwise she had not moved.

She hadn't thought of the window.

A figure, black in the shadow, was moving with infinite stealth over the sill.

"From the porch, of course," thought one part of Susan's mind. "There are stairs somewhere; there must be." And then she realized coldly what a dangerous thing she had undertaken to do.

But it was done, and there she was in Felicia's place. And she must get one clear glimpse of that figure's face.

It was so dark in the shadows by the window. Susan realized she must close her eyes and did so, feigning sleep and listening with taut nerves.

A rustle and a pause.

It was more than flesh and blood could bear. Surely that figure was far enough away from the window by this time so that it could not escape before Susan had a look at its face.

She moved, and there was still silence. She flung one arm outward lazily and sat up as if sleepily and opened her eyes.

"Is that you, Mrs. Denisty?" she asked drowsily.

And looked at the figure and directly into a revolver.

There was to be no pretense then. Susan's vague plan of talk, of excuses on both sides, collapsed.

"If you shoot," she said in a clear low voice that miraculously did not tremble, "the whole house will be here before you can escape."

"I know that." The reply was equally low and clear. "But you know too much, my dear."

The last thing Susan remembered before that pandemonium of struggle began was the revolver being placed quite deliberately upon the green satin eiderdown. Then all knowledge was lost, and she was fighting—fighting for balance, fighting for breath, fighting against blackness, against faintness, against death. If she could get the revolver—but she could not. She could not even gasp for breath, for there were iron hands upon her throat. She twisted and thrust and got free and had a great gasp of air and tried to scream, and then hands were there again, choking the scream.

She kept on pulling at those hands—pulling at something—pulling—but it was easy to drop into that encircling blackness—easy to become part of it—part of it . . .

Somewhere, somehow, in some curious, dim nether world very much time had passed. And someone was insisting that she return, forcing her to come back, making her open her eyes and listen and leave that dizzy place of blackness.

"She's opened her eyes," cried a voice with a curious break in it. Susan stirred, became curious, opened her eyes again, saw a confused circle of faces bending over her, remembered, and screamed:

"Let me go . . . *let me go* . . ."

"It's all right—it's all right, Susan. Look at me. See, I'm Jim. You are all right. Look at me."

She opened her eyes again and knew that Jim was there, and Lieutenant Mohrn and a great many other people. And she knew she was being wrapped in the eiderdown, and that Lieutenant Mohrn and Jim made a sort of a chair with their arms and carried her out of the room and down the stairs. And then all at once she was in Jim's car, warm and snug.

"I'll get the story from her when she's better," said Jim shortly to Lieutenant Mohrn, who stood at the side of the car. Susan, in a very luxury of tears, was crying her heart out.

Jim let her cry and drove very swiftly. His profile looked remarkably grim. He said nothing even when they reached Susan's house, beyond ordering Huldah to fix some hot milk.

The story of the Easter image ended, as, for

Susan, it had begun, in her own small library with a fire blazing cheerfully and the dog at her feet.

"What happened?" she said abruptly.

"Don't talk."

"But I must talk."

He looked at her.

"All right," he said. "But don't talk too much. We got in at the window. Saw the open window on the upper porch and heard—sounds. Got there just in time." He looked back at the fire and was suddenly very grim again.

"Where is—*she?*" whispered Susan.

"Where she belongs. Look here, if you must talk, Sue, how did you know it was that woman? She confessed; had to. She had the gun, you know. The one that killed the butler."

"It couldn't be anyone else," Susan said slowly. "But there wasn't any evidence."

"Huh?" said Jim, in a startled manner.

"I mean," said Susan hurriedly, "there was only my own feeling, the things I saw and heard and felt about the people involved. It was all intangible, you see, until I put the things I knew on paper—chronologically, as they revealed themselves. Then all at once there was a tangible answer. But there weren't ever any direct material clues. Except the gun, there at the last. And the attack upon Felicia."

A paper rustled in Jim's hand.

"Are those my notes?" asked Susan interestedly.

"Yes—Lieutenant Mohrn wanted you to explain them——"

"Very well," she said. "But it's rather like a—a——"

"Problem in algebra," suggested Jim, smiling.

"No," said Susan hastily. She had never been happy with algebraic terms. "It was more like a —a patchwork quilt. Just small unrelated scraps, you know, and a great many of them. And then you put them together in the only way they'll all fit, and there you have a pattern."

Jim read:

"*'Noise in night that must have been crash of Venetian glass and someone brushed my door; thus person breaking glass probably one of household.'* What on earth is that?"

"Part of the campaign against Felicia," said Susan. "It was evident from the first that there was a deliberate and very cruel campaign in progress against Felicia. The glass broken, her flowers dying always (William had said, she told me, something about acid in the water), her kitten, the knitting—it was all part of the plot. Go on."

"'*Why is Felicia the focus of attack?*' Obviously someone wanted her either to do something that she had to be forced to do, or wanted her out of the way entirely."

"Both," said Susan and shivered, "'*Gladstone has a roving eye.*'"

"Kisses maids," said Susan. "Kisses anything feminine in a uniform."

"Did he——" said Jim, threatening.

"Slightly," said Susan, and added hurriedly: "The whole thing, though, was centered about the Easter devil."

"The *what!*" said Jim.

She told him, then, the whole story.

"So you see," she said finally. "It seemed to me that this was the situation. Mrs. Denisty ruled the household, controlled the purse strings, and was against divorce. Someone was deliberately playing on Felicia's nerves by threatening her with the Easter devil and by contriving all sorts of subtle ways of persecution. In this campaign the murder of the butler began to look like nothing more than an incident, for evidently the campaign was continuing. Then, when I found that the bridge had been tampered with (you can see for yourself tomorrow)—there's a place where it is quite evident; the nails holding the planks there in the middle have been taken out and then replaced. It would have been a very bad fall, for it's just over the deepest point of the ravine—and I realized that owing to the French lessons Felicia would have been the first to cross the bridge in the morning, was, in fact, the only one in the household who crossed it daily and at a regular time. I knew thus that the campaign against Felicia had already reached its climax once, and yet had been, for some reason, interrupted."

"Then you think William was murdered because he saw too much?"

"And because he would have told. And his necessary murder, of course, delayed the plot against Felicia. Delayed it until the murderer realized that it could be used as a tool."

"Tool?"

"A reason for what was to appear to be Felicia's suicide."

Jim looked at the paper and read: "'*Dorothy*

*inquires about William; Dorothy seems sincere only when she talks of Mother Denisty ruling the house. Why? Dorothy hints that Mother Denisty knows something of William's murder. Why? Is this smoke screen or sheer hatred of Mrs. Denisty? Dorothy nervous and quick-spoken until I lead her to spot where William was killed; is then poised and calm. Dorothy hints at Felicia becoming suicide. Why?'"*

"Exactly," said Susan. "Why, if not because she's keenly interested in the police inquiry—because she resents Mrs. Denisty's influence, and thus in some way Mrs. Denisty must have opposed Dorothy's own purposes—because she knows too much of the murder herself to permit herself to be anything but extremely guarded and careful in speech and manner when the subject is brought up. When you add up everything, there's just one answer. Just one pattern in which everything fits. And the knitting brought Dorothy directly into it again; that is, none of the family could have pulled out the knitting, the image didn't do it, I felt sure Felicia hadn't, and that left only Dorothy who was free to come and go in the house. But Gladstone pretended publicly that he wasn't afraid of the image, and told Felicia privately that he *was* afraid of it. Believed in its power for evil. You see, Gladstone had to make an issue of something. So he chose the Easter image. It was at the same time a point of disagreement between him and Felicia and a medium through which to work upon Felicia—it's nothing but a painted piece of wood—but I don't like it myself," said Susan. "He couldn't have chosen a better tool. But it was Dorothy who murdered and was ready to murder again."

"Then Gladstone——"

"Gladstone wanted a divorce, but wanted to drive Felicia to ask for it herself, owing to his mother's feeling about divorce. Dorothy had to be in the conspiracy, for she was strongly and directly concerned. But there was this difference: Gladstone (who must have thought he had hit on an exceedingly ingenious plan) only wanted to induce Felicia to leave him. *But Dorothy had other plans.* It wasn't fear that Felicia saw in her eyes: it was hate. I knew that when she talked to me of Felicia's possible suicide. There was the strangest impression that she was paving the way, so to speak; it was then that I realized Felicia's danger. Yet I had no proof. It was, as I said, altogether intangible. Nothing definite. Except, of course, the bridge. If I'd had only one real, material clue I shouldn't have worried so. The footsteps on the bridge, though, were a help, because then I had a link between Dorothy and Gladstone, and I hadn't had that—except intangibly—up till then. But I also realized then that he must have told Dorothy the things Felicia had said to me, that Dorothy would realize that it was dangerous to permit Felicia to talk and that Dorothy would probably act at once. Would carry out the plan that had once been interrupted."

"But you were not sure of this. You had no proof."

"Proof?" said Susan. "Why, no, there was no proof. And no evidence. But I would not have dared deny the evidence of my—intangibles."

Jim grinned rather apologetically at her. "After all," he said. "There's plenty of proof now. They think Dorothy intended to kill Felicia and leave the gun with Felicia's fingerprints on it, thus indicating suicide and also that Felicia had shot the butler herself—hence her possession of the gun, hence also the suicide. Remorse. Of course, there were a hundred ways for Dorothy to have secured the gun."

He paused and looked thoughtfully and soberly into the fire.

"Intangibles," he said presently. "But not so darned intangible after all. But all the same, young woman, you are going to get the worst scolding you ever had in all your life. The *chance* you took——" He stopped abruptly and looked away from Susan, and Susan smoothed back her hair.

"Yes," she said in a small voice. "But I've got to go back there."

"Go back!" cried Jim Byrne explosively. "There?"

"Yes, I forgot to burn the Easter image," said Susan Dare.

The dog grunted and stretched. The fire was warm, the house at peace, the woman at home where she ought to be, and she hadn't seen the scratch on his nose after all.

## The Claret Stick

SUSAN DARE rose from the stage and brushed dust from her skirt. Death in its primary form is never pleasant, and this death was particularly ugly. She felt a queer desire to move the man at her feet so that his battered head no longer hung over into the footlights.

She felt ill and terribly shaken. No wonder that Adelaide Cholster was uttering one hysterical sob after another.

Adelaide Cholster. Susan's eyes went thoughtfully to the small group huddled at the other side of the stage. Adelaide was the faded little blonde —sister, was it?—of the murdered man.

The brown-faced woman in the dark knitted suit, who was so terribly controlled, was his wife, then. Jane they had called her. Jane Cholster.

Susan looked again at the man sprawled upon the stage. He was a large man, heavy but well proportioned. He was blond and probably older than his sister and wife. Of course, the heavy make-up on his mouth and chin was a little confusing.

Susan forced herself to look at his face again. His face was unpowdered, and his eyes had not been touched; his mouth, however, was strongly outlined in soft crimson, and a small beard made of crêpe hair had been fastened to his chin. He had been, then, ready for rehearsal when he was murdered. The blow that had killed him had to be one of enormous power.

"Killed by blunt instrument," thought Susan and looked around the stage. It was set simply for an exterior, a balcony scene, with two long French windows opening at either side upon the balcony of which the footlights defined the limits.

There were a table and two chairs near one of the windows, but neither table nor chairs were heavy enough to deal the blow that had crushed out that hearty, strong life.

She looked again at the small group across the stage. Adelaide was sobbing now in the arms of the slim, dark young man—the one who had called himself Clare Dickenson and whom the others called Dickie.

Jane Cholster was lighting a cigarette, and her brown face, outlined clearly in the small light that the other man was holding for her, looked set. Her full-lipped, strong mouth, however, puffed steadily, her topaz eyes reflected a gleam from the light; Susan realized suddenly that she was an extremely attractive woman, although the charm lay in something aside from beauty. She glanced at the sobbing Adelaide and turned again to the man next her. "How much longer do you think it will be, Tom? Surely, they've had time to find the murderer. He must be somewhere in the theater."

Tom (he had given his name to the constable as Tom Remy, Susan remembered) shrugged and lit a cigarette for himself. "No telling," he said.

Beyond the footlights was a brightly lighted cavern that contained rows and rows of empty seats. Away at the back stood a man on guard— a townsman hastily deputized by the undeniably flustered constable. Below the stage now and then could be heard a rumble of heavy voices, or the bang of a door, or footsteps. They were searching the dressing rooms, the furnace and storage rooms, then.

The Little Theater movement, thought Susan rather dryly, must have been very successful to permit the use of so large a theater—large, at least, for the size of the town. And ambitious! She remembered the placards she had seen in the crowded little drugstore where she and Jim had stopped for directions to reach the theater—large handsomely printed placards announcing the Little Theater's newest production which was to be *Private Lives* and which was to open the following night for a three-night run.

Well, it wouldn't open.

The Cholsters—the murdered man, Jane Cholster, the sister—were all of them exactly the type to go in strongly and rather cleverly for amateur theatricals. They were quite evidently people of means, of leisure, and probably an intelligent understanding of the arts, including the art of play-making.

The man they called Dickie was the director. He would be, then, professional: a man of experience as an actor and a director, paid probably a generous sum by the members of the Little Theater group. He had a thin dark face; clever dark eyes, and an air of quick authoritative efficiency.

Tom Remy, who stood quietly smoking, was a little more difficult to orient. He was tall, stooped, grayish around the temples, and so far had said practically nothing.

All of the faces except the director's showed

signs of make-up, though Jane Cholster had wiped her face thoroughly with her handkerchief. Adelaide lifted her head and sobbed, and Jane Cholster said rather sharply: "Stop that, Adelaide."

"Why don't they get a doctor?" sobbed Adelaide.

"There's no use getting a doctor now," said Tom Remy quietly. "The constable is doing everything he can."

"They're trying to get the murderer before he has a chance to escape," said Dickie quickly and in an efficient manner. "He must be somewhere in the building. The only possible way of escape would have been by the front door, and he didn't go that way."

Adelaide turned a small puffy face, on which heavy make-up was grotesquely streaked with tears, toward the other side of the stage and saw Susan. "Who's that?" she said.

Jane's topaz eyes gave Susan a cool glance.

"She came in with the reporter."

"Reporter!" cried Adelaide. "What reporter?"

"The reporter from the *Record*. He was in Kittiwake for a story about something or other—

spring floods probably, nothing else has happened here—and heard about the murder."

Dickie turned quickly to Tom Remy.

"Oh, is he the fellow that came in with the constable?" His quick clever eyes darted to meet Susan's. "Are you a reporter, too?"

"No. My name is Dare." She looked at Jane. "May I do anything to help you?"

"Nothing, thank you," said Jane. She glanced at the others and said, as if not wholly conscious of them or of Susan: "Miss Cholster. Mr. Remy. Mr. Dickenson."

Something banged heavily below, and Adelaide cried: "What *are* they doing?" There were footsteps on the stairway off toward their right, resounding heavily and rousing dull murmurs that were echoes.

"I wonder if they've found anybody," said Tom Remy. And then the three men were in the wings and approaching the stage again, the constable, red and puffing a bit, in the lead, an assistant (also, Susan suspected, hastily deputized) following him, and Jim Byrne bringing up the rear.

Jim took off his hat, and as the constable, puffing and clutching his revolver, addressed himself to Mrs. Cholster, Jim drew Susan aside.

"My God, Sue," he said under his breath, "what a case! The whole theater's locked up tight. The sheriff's at the other end of the county. And I'll bet my hat the murderer's right here. Have I got a story or have I got a story?"

"You've got a story," said Susan rather somberly. She glanced toward the sprawled gray figure, and Jim caught the look in her eyes. "I know, Sue," he said. "But, after all, it happened."

He stopped abruptly, struck by something the constable was saying, and Susan listened also.

"—And so the sheriff said over the telephone to keep you all here till he got back. He said he'd start right off quick. Now, I'm sorry about this, Mrs. Cholster; but it can't be helped."

"But this is preposterous!" Jane exclaimed. "Do you realize that while you are holding us here my husband's murderer is escaping?"

"Well," said the constable slowly, "we ain't so sure about that."

"What do you mean by that?" she demanded.

"That's easy to answer, ma'am. According to

this Dickenson fellow, nobody went out the front door of the theater. And the stage entrance is bolted on the inside. So it stands to reason that the murderer's still here."

"Do you mean to say that you will not even permit my husband's body to be cared for? I insist upon calling Dr. Marks. And also my lawyer."

"Now, Mrs. Cholster," the constable said, "there ain't no call for you to talk like that. The sheriff said to hold you here, and that's what I'm going to do. He's got to see the body just as it is, and we can't move it till he looks at it and till the coroner looks at it. And I got to go ahead with my inquiry. That's my duty, and I'd advise you folks not to resist the law. I got two deputies here with me, and all of us is armed."

Jane's eyes flashed dangerously. "Did the sheriff say to allow reporters here?" she asked sharply.

"Reporters," said the constable largely, "is always permitted. Dunc, you might take something and cover Mr. Cholster."

Tom Remy stepped forward. "Let's get this straight," he said. "Are you holding us for murder?"

Adelaide blinked and gave a little scream, and the constable said:

"Well, there ain't anybody else around, is there?"

There was, not unnaturally, an abrupt silence. Jane Cholster's face was ashy again under the brown, but set and guarded. Tom Remy's eyes retreated, and Adelaide blinked and gasped and balled her handkerchief at her mouth, and Dickenson's handsome dark face became an impassive mask with only his quick dark eyes alive.

Around them the old theater was very still. Its stage that night already had played a strange and tragic drama, and Susan felt eerily that it was waiting for the play to go on, to play itself out. Below were passages and empty dressing rooms. Above was a dim loft extending mysteriously upward.

The constable's voice broke the silence. "I reckon," he said, "I'd better ask you some questions. And I reckon I don't need to tell you that you'd better tell the truth. Now, then, there's some chairs back there somewhere. Dunc," he continued "bring them out. We may as well be comfortable." The little deputy disappeared, and the constable turned and shouted toward the bulky, dark figure standing at the back of the house. "Don't let anybody in, Wid, till the sheriff gets here."

"Here's a chair, miss," said Dunc's small voice to Susan, and she accepted it.

She looked at the other people seating themselves in a kind of circle on the stage.

Was Jane Cholster's character so strong that she could indefinitely withhold any signs of grief and shock? Was Adelaide so loving and so tender that she must collapse frequently into sobs? Was either of these women physically strong enough to deal the crushing blow that had been dealt Brock Cholster?

Jane was slender and brown and looked as if her muscles were hard. She must have, too, a tremendous reserve of nerve power. She sat now quietly erect and graceful—but under her quiet you felt that muscles might be gathered ready to spring.

Jane was only of medium height, but Adelaide looked small beside her. She huddled in the armchair that the deputy had given her. Her faded blonde curls were pushed up away from her puffy little face. She was older than Susan had surmised, for there were definite little pouches under her eyes and in the corners of her chin. Susan was vaguely aware that Jim and the constable were talking in a low murmur, there near the body; her eyes traveled on to the nervous, dark young director and to Tom Remy.

Either of the men might have been physically capable of that blow, providing a suitable weapon were at hand. ("Weapon?" thought Susan parenthetically. "What happened to it? And what *was* it?")

Neither, however, looked exactly athletic, although you couldn't measure the strength that sheer emotion might give to inadequate muscular force.

Tom Remy was smoking again; his eyes were narrowed into lines that made them look sharp and very observant and yet altogether unfathomable. As Susan watched, he gave Jane Cholster a long look which she returned, and Susan had a curious feeling that there was an unspoken communication between them, although neither face changed at all.

The dark young director passed a hand over his smooth black hair and said suddenly: "Who put the curtain up?"

"Curtain?" said Jane slowly. The constable turned abruptly to join the small circle, and Jim followed him, and the man Dickenson said quickly:

"Curtain, of course. It was down when I arrived, for I glanced at the stage. I didn't put it up. Who did?"

No one replied, and the constable said:

"What's all this about a curtain? You mean the fire curtain? It's a village ordinance that it——"

"Exactly. Of course. I know." Dickenson's interruptions were sharp and quick. "Certainly it was down. And when I came out of the office down there—" he motioned, with the nervous quickness that characterized his gestures, toward the door leading to the foyer—"and walked up here, the curtain was up."

"It was you that discovered the body?"

"Of course. You know that. I told you when I telephoned for you."

"When did you know it was Mr. Cholster?"

"I—" he closed his eyes for an instant as if to recall and Susan could see a little flutter of his eyeballs under his thin dark lids—"I believe I was only aware that the curtain was up and that there was something humped up there. But I hurried up to the switchboard and turned on the lights and saw it was Mr. Cholster. I thought, of course, he'd fainted or something and ran out on the stage. And I stopped about there and knew —what had happened."

"Then what did you do?"

"I—I think I called out. Everybody else, you know, was downstairs getting ready for rehearsal. Then I ran back to the telephone in the office again. When I came out, Tom and Mrs. Cholster and Adelaide were all on the stage——"

"You had the main door locked when I got here," said the constable. "How was that? When did you lock it?"

"I had locked it as soon as everybody got here. Locked it simply because we needed a good last rehearsal, and if I had left the door unlocked we'd have been continually interrupted. A lot of Kittiwake residents prefer sneaking in to dress rehearsal to coming around the next night and paying for their tickets."

Jim cleared his throat gently, and the constable cleared his also and said politely: "Did you say something, Mr. Byrne?"

"I was only wondering," said Jim, "why you didn't use the stage entrance. It would seem more convenient."

"Well, it isn't," said the young director rather snappishly. "There's no key to the thing extant, and you have to bolt it on the inside. It's bolted now."

"Then the only exit for the murderer was the door that the deputy is guarding now?"

"Yes," said Dickenson.

"And the door to the office is just at right angles to it there in the foyer, isn't it?"

"Yes, of course."

"Then you must have seen anyone entering or leaving the theater?"

"Why, I—" His quick dark eyes swept around the circle and he said—"that's what I thought when you first questioned me. But I suppose I could have been mistaken."

The constable cleared his throat again and looked at Jim, who said:

"I hope you don't mind letting me get this straight? You told the constable you arrived at the theater at about twenty minutes to eight?"

"Yes."

"You had called a dress rehearsal at eight?"

"I had said make-up at eight sharp. Rehearsal at eight-fifteen."

"Was it customary to make up for dress rehearsal?" asked Jim, Irish honey on his tongue. "I thought that was only to get used to properties—all that."

"Well," said the director hesitating, "it is. But you see—" he paused, and then said with abrupt candor—"but you know how it is with amateurs. They like the smell of grease paint." Dickenson stopped rather short and said: "Are you conducting this inquiry or getting a story for your paper?"

Jim said: "You unlocked the theater when you arrived?"

"Certainly. That is, I unlocked that one door."

"Who arrived next?"

"Jane—Mrs. Cholster, and—Brock. They came together."

Jim turned to Jane Cholster.

"Mrs. Cholster, do you know of anything that was worrying your husband? Was he quite as usual tonight?"

"Quite," said Jane Cholster steadily. "He was a little sleepy, owing to having been gardening most of the afternoon. If you are trying to make out that my husband had any enemies, you are wasting your time. He had none."

The constable spoke suddenly. "Now, Mrs.

Cholster," he said, "you and Miss Adelaide, there, living so close to him all in the same house —and Mr. Remy the next-door neighbor—between you, you ought to be able to give some sort of helpful evidence. This murder had a motive. It wasn't an accident. And it wasn't robbery. Nothing's been taken from Mr. Cholster. You'd ought to be more helpful, Mrs. Cholster."

"*But I tell you—*" Jane paused to control the impatience in her voice—"I tell you there is nothing," she said. "Nothing. He was in no quarrel. He had no enemies."

"The village has it that he's a rich man."

"Not rich," said Jane. "He was no millionaire."

"Did he leave any insurance?"

"Really, Mr. Lambrikin," said Jane, the dangerous light flaring in her eyes again. "You'll have to ask our lawyer about that. I can tell you, however, that my husband was always very generous with me and with Adelaide. It is true that he controlled all the Cholster money—my money and Adelaide's inheritance, as well as his own. But he gave us anything we wanted. His will is no secret either: our own money was to revert to each of us and to each of us half of

Brock's estate. I assure you that there is no motive for murder there. If either of us wanted money we had only to ask for it at any time."

"After Mr. and Mrs. Cholster arrived at the theater, what happened? Did they stop to speak to you?" It was Jim again, all his Celtic grace so smoothly to the fore that even Dickenson did not question his right to inquire.

"They stopped there in the doorway, and we chatted a moment. Then they said they were going down to the dressing rooms to make up, and Brock said he'd decided it would change his appearance more to an audience of townspeople if he wore a beard, and he'd got one already made. He handed Mrs. Cholster his make-up box and cap, and she went on into the theater while Brock showed me the beard—it's there on his chin now—and then he went on."

"I arrived next," said Tom Remy suddenly. "I stopped, too, and spoke to Dickie, and then went directly through the house—up those steps and, without even glancing out on the stage, to the dressing rooms. The stage was dark. And I do remember that the curtain was down."

"Did you see the Cholsters downstairs?" asked the constable quickly.

"I saw Mrs. Cholster," said Tom Remy slowly. "She stood there in her dressing-room door. I spoke to her a moment and went on to my own dressing room. But I do not believe that Mrs. Cholster left her dressing room at all until we heard Dickie shouting for us from up here."

"Why do you think that?" said Jim.

"Because," said Tom Remy, "I could hear her voice."

"Her voice?" cried the constable. "You mean she was talking to somebody? That would be Mr. Cholster, then. Was that——"

"No," said Jane. "I was not talking to my husband. I never saw him again alive after I left him at the door of the office back there." She stopped—deliberately, Susan thought—after throwing out the word "office." The constable's eyes went to Dickenson, who looked suddenly white.

Jim said: "To whom were you talking, Mrs. Cholster?"

Susan caught a tiny flame in Jane's eyes. She said: "I was rehearsing my lines."

Dickenson had got his breath.

"If you think that I killed Brock and dragged him up here to the stage you are wrong. I couldn't have lifted him. It's physically impossible."

"Maybe," said the constable. "But as to that, I don't know as any of you could have lifted him. Or struggled with him, for that matter. He was easy stronger than any one of you. Any one of you." He looked speculative and added: "Of course, two of you——"

"The wound," said Jim in a voice without any inflection at all, "was in the forehead. Somebody had to be very close to him. And directly in front of him. Therefore someone he knew and did not fear."

Jane leaped to her feet. "How dare you say such things! It is not true."

"Jane—Jane——" said Tom Remy, with again a guarded note of warning in his voice. "Look here, Constable, I am sure that Mrs. Cholster was in her dressing room downstairs from the time I arrived to the time we heard Dickie shouting for us here on the stage."

"We ain't saying Mrs. Cholster is the murderer," said the constable. "But Brock Cholster's dead, ain't he? Now then, Dickenson, you claimed that you saw everybody that entered the theater tonight."

"I thought so," he said rapidly. "But now that I've had time to think of it I realize that someone might have entered without my knowledge——"

"You said you were in the office the whole time from your arrival till everybody was here. Who came last? Miss Adelaide?"

"Yes, Adelaide. Yes, I said that in the haste of the moment when you arrived, Constable. But now I realize that someone must have slipped past the office door when I wasn't looking."

"And then slipped out again after he'd murdered Brock Cholster?" inquired the constable heavily.

"Exactly," said Dickenson eagerly. "That's what must have happened. There's no other explanation."

"It's pretty late for it, Dickenson," said the constable. "And it ain't reasonable to suppose that you saw everybody else that entered the theater and were sitting right there by the door from the time you unlocked it until you locked it again, and yet the murderer got past you twice without your seeing him. No, it ain't reasonable. Now, Miss Adelaide, what's your story?"

"Why, I—I came in, as Dickie said. And I

went along the aisle there at the side and up those steps—just as the others did, I suppose, and then immediately down to my dressing room. That's all I know. That is, till I heard Dickie calling for us up here on the stage, and we all hurried upstairs and saw—" she gave a convulsive shudder and finished—"saw him."

"Was the curtain up when you came along the aisle?"

She blinked, hesitated, and then was certain. "I don't know. I really don't know. I don't remember it at all."

"Was the stage dark?"

"Yes. Yes, it must have been."

Jim coughed lightly, and the constable looked at him, and Jim said: "Odd that no one heard any noise——"

"Did anyone hear a noise?" asked the constable directly.

No one replied, and the small silence grew oppressive. Again Susan was acutely conscious of the empty waiting theater, of the spaces, of the shadows, of the empty passages and rooms below them. Behind them, of course, was the balcony set with its French doors, and wings jutting out that looked like brick walls with vines over them.

She glanced up and over her shoulder into what she could see of the loft. It, too, was dim in spite of lights, and hung with great ghostly ropes that stretched hazily upward into darkness.

She wondered if anyone could conceal himself up there in the dim reaches of the loft, clinging somehow to perilous ropes, and decided that it was not possible. She did not, however, like those mysterious dark spaces above and out in the wings.

The constable sighed and said: "Mrs. Cholster, didn't you hear anything?"

Jane Cholster moistened her lips.

"I heard nothing like—like a blow," she said as if forcing out the words. "I did hear someone on the stage. Arranging it, I thought, and supposed it was Mr. Dickenson. I didn't give it much attention."

"Mr. Remy?"

"Why, I—I didn't hear anything like a blow, either. Could we have heard that?"

The constable glanced toward the heap under its covering and said: "I think you could have heard it. Did you hear anyone on the stage?"

"I don't know," said Tom Remy. "I remember thinking that Dickie was getting the stage ready, but I don't know why I thought that—must have heard some sound, I suppose. Certainly," he added, as if making amends to Dickenson, "I had no reason to think it was Dickenson except that he usually arranged the stage for us. And it was only a vague recognition of someone moving about above us. Then there was, too, a sort of rumbling sound."

"A rumbling sound——"

"That was the ventilator," said Dickenson at once. "I had turned it on—the switch is in the office—to see how it worked. It's a recent addition and wasn't made for old theaters. It makes a lot of noise here. We can only use it between acts and when the theater is empty. But I was not arranging the stage."

"What time was the ventilator going?"

"I don't know exactly. Around eight, I suppose."

"Did *you* hear anything? Anything besides the—ventilator?"

"No," said Dickenson. "Nothing. But I'd like to know who put the curtain up."

Again no one spoke, and again the old theater waited. Someone behind Susan sighed: it was the little deputy. Jane Cholster was biting her lips, and Adelaide was staring upward in her turn into the mysterious ghostly reaches of the fly loft. Tom Remy blew out beige smoke, and quite suddenly there was a small skittering sound. Though it was faint, everyone started.

Then Dickenson said softly: "Mice," and Adelaide screamed raggedly but softly and pulled up her feet and jerked her skirt tighter over her legs.

Mere nerves, of course. They were all terribly aware, as Susan herself was aware, that murder had walked that stage.

And the murderer was still at large—or at least still undiscovered. Which of those taut, unrevealing faces concealed murder?

Or was it possible that the search of the theater had left some dark corner unseen?

"Then some time between ten minutes till eight and ten minutes after eight the murder occurred," said the constable suddenly. "Did you say they were to put this stuff on their faces at eight, Dickenson?"

Dickenson shrugged.

"Oh—I said make-up at eight," he said. "But that doesn't mean that Brock Cholster went down to his dressing room at exactly eight and then came up here again."

"But he was in his dressing room at some time," pressed the constable.

"Must have been."

"And he was murdered after he was made up?"

"Well, obviously. And obviously he wasn't murdered in his dressing room. Nobody could have got him up that stairway."

"When was your husband in his dressing room, Mrs. Cholster?"

"I—don't know."

"You didn't hear him at all?"

"No."

"But you know Mr. Remy was there?"

It was then that the storm growing behind Jane Cholster's lambent eyes burst into fury. She rose with a lithe movement and faced the constable.

"Constable," she said furiously. "This is an outrage. You are keeping us in this horrible place, frightening us—inquiring; and we have no recourse but to stay here and wait for the sheriff. But we can refuse to talk, and I do so now. I will not answer another question. And I will wait for the sheriff how and where I please."

She whirled and walked off the stage, turning aside beyond the switchboard. They could hear her quick footsteps as she went down the steps leading to the outside aisle of the house.

"Hey, there," cried the constable, standing. "You can't leave."

The trim dark figure did not turn. They watched as she coolly selected a seat and sat down in it, leaning her head on her hand.

Tom Remy, Adelaide, and Dickenson had risen, too, as if Jane's action had inspired them also to defiance, and were drifting toward the wings, Adelaide supported solicitously by the sleek young director.

"Well, let 'em go," said the constable to the deputy, who looked troubled. "Guess there's nothing much to do but wait for the sheriff."

"What do you think of it?" said Jim.

"Well," said the constable, "looks very much as if the deed was done around eight o'clock. Probably between eight and eight-ten. I figure it took Mr. Cholster a few minutes to get that stuff on his face. Then for some reason he came back here on the stage. Mr. Remy and Mrs. Cholster sort of alibi each other, but alibis ain't always certain. Miss Adelaide didn't hardly have time to kill him without an awful lot of luck before this Dickenson fellow locked the door and came straight up to the stage. I figure it wasn't more than a minute. I——"

"What's that?" It was Dickenson beside them suddenly, and Jim said:

"The constable and I were just saying that you must have followed Miss Adelaide into the theater almost at once."

"I did. I spoke to her, and she came on in, and I turned off the ventilator, locked the door, and followed."

"She must have put on her make-up very quickly," said Susan.

Dickenson's quick dark eyes gave her a very sharp look.

"Why, yes, I suppose she was hurrying. Probably hadn't finished when I found Cholster and called. If you're figuring whether she had time to —to kill him and then get down to her dressing room and get make-up on, why she didn't. And I realize that that leaves me the only one without an alibi; but I didn't kill him."

The constable said something again about the uncertainty of alibis, and Susan drifted away.

No one looked at the small figure in brown that unobtrusively crossed the stage, rounded the end of the set, and found herself in the dim world backstage. Now Susan could see the fly loft more clearly, though it was still a mysterious dark realm draped in a ghostly etching of ropes. Away up there were—what did they call them? Grids, was it?—great pulleys, anyway, over which the ropes passed. And nearer but still far away, flys and borders and drops and even empty battens were hanging motionless in the musty air. A theater has, as if distilled within it, a life of its own, and Susan, standing backstage, was strongly aware of that sentience. Voices drifted to her, and Susan turned and made her way toward the railed stairway that descended to the dressing rooms.

The air was colder and felt dank, and the musty smells were heavier. As she reached the last step she reminded herself that the whole place had been thoroughly searched.

The narrow passage ran up and down, with doors opening from it. It was lighted, of course; they had turned on every light in the theater. The light, however, rather emphasized its dreariness. There were six dressing rooms. Two of them were empty; the other four had, each of them, a make-up box on the table below the mirror. Susan entered swiftly one after another.

The first was probably Adelaide's, for a beige coat was flung hurriedly over the chair, and the top layer of the make-up box (Susan paused to remark the extremely nice make-up box that Adelaide had chosen to supply herself with for use merely as an amateur) had been removed, as if hastily, and lay on the bare table with its sticks of grease paint spilling. Pink powder lay open, also spilling, and a box of rouge. Susan looked carefully at the many sticks and pencils—liners, weren't they called?—and their colors and went on to the next dressing room. It was empty except for a gray cap and a make-up box—the make-up box was open and was much like Adelaide's. Because of the cap, Susan felt reasonably certain that it was the room the dead man was supposed to have used.

The other two dressing rooms were across the narrow passage and past an expanse of whitewashed wall and were not directly opposite the first two rooms. The first one held another handsome make-up box, identical with the other two. It was closed, but there was a towel on the table with wisps of powder on it, and two or three cigarette ends and ashes were on the floor. Probably that was Jane's room, and she had apparently finished her make-up and closed the box. In the remaining room there was no make-up box at all, although on the table lay a box of tan powder, a black eyebrow liner, and a stick of carmine lip paste. Tom Remy, then, used only the barest essentials. Susan pulled her loose pigskin glove over her hand and picked up the stick of lip paste. And just then something flickered in the wavery mirror before her.

Susan stared and whirled.

The doorway was bare and there was only whitewashed wall opposite. Surely there had been a motion there at the door. Surely—she put down the carmine paste and was at the door. The passage was dreary and empty.

But she realized suddenly that she could no longer hear voices from above.

Well, she had seen what she came to see. She would return. The passage, however, was rather dark. And certainly very quiet. And the door to the room that had had the gray tweed cap in it was closed.

She stopped abruptly.

She had left it open. She was sure of that.

Quite suddenly and absurdly, she was frightened and wanted to scream. And just then there was a rustle in the room and a quick metallic click. The door swung wide, and Tom Remy stood on the threshold and saw her.

He said calmly: "Oh, Miss—er—Dare. You look frightened."

"I—I didn't know you were here," said Susan.

His eyes retreated to dark, enigmatic slits, and for a long moment he stood there looking at her. Then he said finally and very slowly: "Yes, I—I came down to get Miss Adelaide's coat."

"What is your profession, Mr. Remy?" She was relieved to find that her question sounded quite steady.

"I'm a painter."

"Landscape?" inquired Susan.

"Portraits," he said. "Why?"

"There's a beige coat in the dressing room nearest the stairs," said Susan. "Did you——"

A figure emerged rather promptly from Adelaide's dressing room. It had the beige coat over its arm and was Dickenson. He looked at them and said: "I've got her coat, Tom."

"Why, I—" said Tom Remy and stopped abruptly and said: "Oh, I see."

Which was it, thought Susan, preceding the two men up the stairway, who had been watching her? And why? At the top of the stairs she paused to look at the door that was the stage entrance.

"Here, Tom," said Dickenson suddenly. "Take this coat on to Adelaide, will you? I'll—er—be there in a minute, tell her."

"All right," said Remy briefly.

"This is the stage entrance?" murmured Susan.

"Certainly. Bolted up tight. Not even the cat could get in."

"Of course," said Susan. "I see. She looked at the bolt, then lifted it and put her gloved hand on the under side of the heavy latch. The door opened, and night air swept in, and a stalwart figure loomed out of the darkness beyond.

"Hey, there," it said truculently. "Shut that door and stay in there, miss."

"Well guarded," said Dickenson. His thin lips smiled, but his eyes looked worried, and Susan let the bolt fall back into place. He turned as she turned, and walked toward the stage beside her.

"That," said Susan, "is, of course, the switchboard?" She indicated the panel set into the wall.

He nodded. "Here's the signal for the asbestos curtain," he volunteered. "It's the only curtain or drop in the theater that's controlled by an electric switch. The rest of these are lights."

She walked out on the stage. Jane Cholster was still sitting coolly in the seat she had chosen. Tom Remy was bending over her, and both were talking.

Adelaide, wrapped now in her beige coat, was sitting near them, staring at nothing.

Away at the back, the constable was having a conference with the deputy on guard at the door. The other deputy—Dunc—was sitting on the stage looking thin and disconsolate. Jim was nowhere to be seen.

Susan approached the deputy, and he sprang up with a startled look and put his hand on his revolver. Dickenson was watching her from the wings with steady, knowing black eyes. She said in a low voice to the deputy: "Have any of those people down there moved about the theater much?"

"Huh?" He had pale blue eyes which opened in surprise. "No, I guess not. That is, Tom Remy went downstairs a few minutes ago. And this young Dickenson fellow, too."

"Which one first?"

"Dickenson, I think."

Susan said slowly: "I believe that one of them is going to try to hide something. Something that's important. Do you——"

"Sure! I get it! I'll watch every move they make." His eyes had lighted up, and her tone must have carried conviction, for he did not question her, which was as well, for Dickenson was crossing the stage to her side. She turned toward the French doors, and again he turned with her, followed her as she went through them and stopped when she stopped.

Furniture for a drawing room was crowded in space between the two sets. A light couch, several chairs, a table.

"It's for the second act," said Dickenson, watching her. Curious, said something in the back of Susan's mind, how quickly we are removed from the deputy—from the people sitting out there in the house. It's almost as if we were entirely alone. She moved a little away from the slender, dark figure but he moved also. She was acutely conscious of his dark eyes, and of his shoulder all but touching her own as she bent closer to scrutinize the couch.

"They looked here for a weapon, I suppose," she said.

"Yes, I—I think so."

She moved around the couch, and he followed her. She was aware of his silent graceful tread behind her as she walked out into the wings again and around behind the second act set. She was plunged at once into a dark world of empty spaces that seemed, somehow, not empty. She looked up again into the shadowy loft.

Against the dark old wall and about thirty feet above the stage was a small wooden platform. Narrow wooden steps led upward to it, and ropes from away overhead dropped in long taut lines to its railing . . . Susan turned toward it, and the man at her side said suddenly:

"See here, you aren't going up in the fly gallery, are you?"

"Why not?" said Susan, wondering what he would say.

"Well, it's—it's against union rules, you know. Nobody but stage crew is permitted up there. And—and then there must be two men; I mean to manipulate the ropes, you know. It's—rather dangerous. Nearly had an accident myself once —fellow let down what looked like an empty rope, not realizing it held a weight. Came very near to hitting me. Since then, believe me, I warn my casts to stay away from the gallery. These amateurs —— I say, what in the world do you want to go up there for? There's nothing there."

He wasn't as quick-witted as somehow she had expected him to be; otherwise his objections would have been more forceful.

She put her hand on the railing of the steps and was glad it was there, for Susan had never liked a ladder or anything remotely resembling it.

"Union rules aren't applying tonight," she said lightly and started upward.

It was not a pleasant climb. The steps were very narrow and very steep, and she was altogether too acutely aware that he was still following her. Step by step, just there below her heels. Oh, well—she could always call out to the people below. That is, if there were need. But she rather wished she had waited for Jim.

And when she reached the small gallery it seemed very much farther to the floor of the stage than the same distance had seemed looking up. She closed her eyes against a momentary dizziness and clung to the heavy railing.

"If you're looking for clues," said Dickenson's suave voice at her side, "there's nothing at all here. Don't you think you'd better go down again? I can't have you fainting on my hands up here."

Susan opened her eyes.

"I'm not fainting," she said. "What are these things called?" She touched one of a line of long wooden pegs fastened along the railing, from which extended the ropes.

"Pins," he said briefly. "Ropes pass over those pulleys up there and are looped in a half-hitch around these. Holds them. It takes an expert to manipulate these things. The flys and drops are very heavy, you know. The new theaters have everything controlled by electricity. It's grand when you get in a place like that." His eyes slid toward her face, and he said: "I shouldn't dare to work one of these myself; though, of course, I've done it now and then in rehearsals. But the weight is much heavier than you'd think. Knew of a fellow once that got his ankle twisted in one of the coils, the thing got away from him, and he was carried clear up to the grids—an eighty-foot drop below." He looked at her more fully and said very slowly and markedly: "It's very dangerous."

*He knows that I know*, thought Susan.

She looked downward. The back part of the stage was spread out below her as if it were on a platter. But the exterior set and the border above it cut off, except for a band of brighter light, a view of the deputy and of the seats. There were people near—yet no one was to be seen. And no one knew where she was.

It looked a long distance to the floor below. How easy an accident would be—how easy a slip and a fall!

It was just then that she saw the loops of rope. The loops that were not quite like those other loops—the loops that were irregular and lacked entirely the sureness that marked those about the other pins. For her life she could not have refrained from putting out her hand and clutching the rope above that pin.

"Look out," said Dickenson in a swift hard voice.

Susan was looking upward through the dimness of the loft. It was dust that made it so dim —a lazy fog of dust hanging up there, moving in its own mysterious course. What did that rope support in the midst of the masking dusk?

Dickenson's hands, like steel, were on her own. "Stop that," he said. And then Susan knew that someone was moving on the floor below. It was a small figure in a beige coat, and it looked up and said: "Dickie. Dickie, darling, what *are* you doing?"

Susan could feel Dickenson's muscles jerk at the sound of Adelaide's voice. But he did not relinquish his grip, although he called out in a strange voice:

"Go back to Jane, Adelaide. And stay there. Go on——"

But Adelaide too was staring upward into the purple fog of dust. Susan, fascinated, watched her small face become rigid and her eyes become fixed and black and horrified.

"*Dickie*——" screamed Adelaide and turned blindly and fell in a huddled queer heap.

Dickenson released Susan's hands and was climbing down the steps. The deputy reached Adelaide first, and then Jane came hurrying from somewhere, and Tom Remy followed. By the time they had moved Adelaide to the couch and pushed things about to give her air, the constable and Jim were there, too.

Susan clung to the railing and watched. The figures below were foreshortened and queer, but every word floated up to her ears.

So that was the weapon. But what was the motive?

Her knees were unsteady, and she glanced at the steep narrow steps at her side and did not want to undertake that descent. It was always easier to climb a ladder than to go down it again. Jim, below, was looking for her.

She whistled softly, and he saw her, though no one else looked away from the couch where Adelaide was lying. His eyes looked relieved, and he walked directly under the gallery and said softly:

"Come down."

Susan looked at the ladder-like steps again and shook her head. "Can't."

He started to speak, stopped, and decided to join her. Her breath began to come more evenly as she watched his gray shoulders come nearer and nearer.

He emerged onto the gallery and said rather grimly: "I was looking for you."

"And high time," said Susan unsteadily. "Take a girl for a ride, plunge her into murder, and leave her there, scared half to death."

"Nonsense," said Jim simply. "See here, Susan, what do you make of all this? And why did that woman down there faint?"

"Because I know what the weapon was that killed Brock Cholster," said Susan. "And she knows, too."

"Weapon?" said Jim.

Susan looked at the couch and then upward again into the purple dusk.

"Jim," she said slowly. "I'm going to put myself in the place of the murderer for a moment. And I want you to listen. Suppose I want to murder Brock Cholster—perhaps have wanted to for a long time, or perhaps quite suddenly want to more overwhelmingly than I have ever wanted to before. Suppose I come up on the stage and the asbestos curtain is down and thus no one can see and for some reason I stop there and discover that Cholster is there, too. That he is sleepy and drowsy, for he's been gardening all day—that he is lying at full length on the couch down there."

"Susan——"

"Wait. I stand there perhaps and look at him and hate him. Hate him as I've never done before. Hate him until it is almost insupportable. For he stands in the way of something I must have. And I wish that he were dead. But the wish isn't enough to kill him, and perhaps it's accident

—or perhaps it's some memory of danger from above that makes me look upward. And way up there, hanging like a sword of Damocles I see a weapon—wait, Jim, don't talk——

"It's hanging there as if it were waiting for me. And it looks as if Cholster has actually chosen to put himself directly under it—as if fate itself were offering the weapon ready for my hand. I look at it and think only of that weapon at last ready for me and that no one will know—or dream of looking up there. There isn't much time, so I hurry up to this gallery. And I find the rope that holds that weight. So I—I let down the rope—slowly, perhaps, *until I discover that it is actually*, as it looked from down there, *directly above his head*. And when I'm sure of that I let it fall. Heavily."

She stopped and this time Jim did not offer to speak. He was staring upward, and his face looked white and grim. He said finally: "And then what?"

"Then," said Susan. "I jerked the thing up again. I loop the rope hurriedly around this pin. I hurry down the steps. He is dead, and the thing is done. Suddenly the nervous tension of that awful emotion collapses, and I am terrified. How can I hide my own part in what has happened? How can I confuse things—make them seem different—somehow change things? The lack of a weapon will lead suspicion away from the people now in the theater and thus from myself. Fortunately he is on the couch, and the couch—Jim, you remember the rumbling sound they heard?"

Jim looked at her. "The ventilator?"

"Perhaps it was going, too, but the sound of someone arranging the stage was the sound of that light couch being pushed across the stage. (It's got casters and would move readily; I looked to be sure.) It would not be difficult to pull the body off the couch and return the couch to its place. And as the body lay when it was discovered, there was nothing but proscenium and ceiling above it, for it was far out over the footlights. It was simple enough to put up the absestos curtain and thus allow the body to project beyond the curtain line."

Jim shook his head slowly.

"But the murderer couldn't have known that Cholster would be exactly there."

"The murderer *didn't* know! Of course, he didn't know. That's the key to the whole affair.

The crime wasn't planned at all. All that stored-up hatred didn't, perhaps, even reach the point of murder until the murderer saw the man and the weapon. Victim and weapon together, at a time when for some reason the murderer was worked up to a frenzy—all three combined like chemicals and produced murder."

Susan's grave low voice came to a stop. In the silence, she could hear the crisp flap of a newspaper with which Jane was fanning Adelaide and the murmur of Tom Remy's voice speaking to Dickenson.

Jim sighed and said very soberly and deliberately:

"I believe you're right, Sue. The weight will show it under analysis. And of course, if it didn't come exactly over his head it would have been a simple matter to fasten the rope, run down to him without waking him and swing the thing so that it—accomplished its purpose. The weight itself isn't much, but the momentum makes it deadly. Yes, Sue, I think you're right. But any one of them could have done it. Who had a motive?"

"The motive must have been actually desire," said Susan slowly. "Desire so strong that it produced a smoldering, gathering hatred. All ready to be lashed into frenzy. But I don't know." She paused, wishing she could seek objectively instead of subjectively through all those currents of feeling and motives and consciousness that are handily put together and labeled personality. Or character. Jim was more reasonable and more definite than she was; she could only push out blind tentacles of something that was perilously like intuition.

"I don't know," she said sadly, "what that lashing was."

Jim said thoughtfully: "Revenge might come into it. A grudge. The constable says Cholster had really a wicked temper. Town gossip has it that he was nothing short of a tyrant in his own home."

"Does the constable's knowledge extend to Jane Cholster's reaction?"

"I asked about that. He knew of nothing, except that she was a bit high-handed. But if there was trouble between them, the constable hadn't heard of it. Oh, by the way, Sue—this young Dickenson isn't altogether honest in his statement about what he was doing back there in the office. He was actually talking over long distance."

"Talking!"

"Exactly. To some woman. I went back to telephone my story. Had to make a long distance call, and the girl asked if I wanted the charge reversed again. I said, 'Again?' and she said, 'Oh I thought it was Mr. Dickenson. You're at the Majestic, aren't you?' (The Majestic, dear Susan, is the name of this theater.) It took only a minute or two to get it out of her. At ten minutes to eight o'clock he was talking to a girl in Springfield. It lasted only a few minutes, so it isn't an alibi. And from what central, who obligingly listened in, says, it was an extremely loving conversation. Why are you looking so queer?"

"Queer?" said Susan vaguely. "Oh—nothing. Except that there's the weapon, you see. And the murderer. And—odd, isn't it, if that telephone conversation hadn't taken place there would have been no murder."

"What——"

"Oh, yes, of course. It couldn't have been any other way. But—oh, look—look, Jim, quick—down there! See, she's becoming conscious again. She's opening her eyes—she's looking—she's remembering."

Jim, watching, saw the figure in the beige coat

stir, sit upright, and fumble suddenly at the bottom of the coat.

Susan was leaning forward, her face white and her eyes frightened.

"Quick, Jim, get the coat. Somehow—anyhow——"

After all, she did not even remember going down that narrow, steep flight of steps. She didn't know either what Jim said to the others. She only knew that he thrust the coat into her hands.

The pockets were empty, but she found it in the bottom of the coat between the lining and the soft beige wool. She worked the small hard object up until it emerged from a torn bit of the lining of a pocket and was in her fingers.

"What are you doing?" demanded Jane Cholster. Her face was pasty gray and her eyes blazing.

Susan did not reply. Instead she crossed the stage, and Jim was beside her when she knelt there at the body. It was he who thrust Tom Remy out of the way when he would have snatched at the thing that Susan held. Somebody —the constable it was—seized Remy and held him struggling, and the guard at the door and the little deputy were both running toward them.

Then Susan covered the face again.

"What——" Said Jim. "Who did it?"

Susan felt ill and wished she had never heard of Kittiwake. She said to Jane: "Did you put the make-up box and cap in his dressing room?"

"Yes, of course," said Jane slowly. "I left it open and ready for him."

"You knew that he objected," said Susan after a long moment. "You knew he refused."

"God forgive me," said Jane suddenly looking old and tired. "I knew—I think we all knew——"

Susan nodded to Jim. "I wasn't sure," she said, "until Mrs. Cholster admitted it just now. That is, I wasn't sure of the motive. The rest of it was terribly simple."

She held out her hand toward the constable. "Here it is," she said. "The lipstick that was used on his mouth by the murderer."

"Lip—" said the constable and after a long time added—"stick." And away at the back someone was suddenly pounding on the doors—pounding so loud that the sound echoed in waves that all but submerged those on the stage.

The constable turned to the deputy. "Open the door for the sheriff," he said.

The group moved and wavered. The sound and motion left Jim and Susan for a moment as if on a small remote island.

"Are you sure?" said Jim.

Susan nodded. "The face was made up for only one motive, and that had to be to give the impression that it had been made up before the murder; thus that the murder had been done after, approximately, eight o'clock—the time set for make-up. Therefore, it must have been done before eight or thereabouts. Therefore it had to be done by someone who was here at eight—Dickenson—Jane—Tom Remy."

"Wait. How do you know the face was made up by the murderer?"

"There was no powder on it and no cream. That would have been put on first. And the lipstick on his mouth was not matched in color or in quality by any of the lip paste in the make-up boxes downstairs. Of course, there were a hundred places to hide the lipstick. But it was not hidden till too late."

The pounding stopped and there was a sound of voices—inquiring, explaining.

Jim glanced over Susan's shoulder and said tersely: "Go on. Quick."

"Well, then—since the murder wasn't planned, there must be inconsistencies—things that changed somehow in the very act of being done. Blunders. I tried again to follow what I should have done in the murderer's place: frantic, trying to confuse things again—changing the position of the body, putting on the beard—Cholster had it there in his hand, probably, and it must have suggested that attempt at make-up. Yet there was no time to open a make-up box and do it thoroughly. Besides, the powder would have spilled. The beard and lipstick were enough, anyway."

"Yes—yes——"

"Well, then, I would have turned and—and passed the switchboard and put up the asbestos curtain—perhaps, as I said before, so the body could be dragged out near the footlights, perhaps merely from that frantic blind desire to confuse, to make things opposite to what they had been. I don't know. But after that I would have gone down to the dressing room. And *on the way* I would have passed the stage entrance. And I would have known suddenly of another change—

of another inconsistency. That I could walk out that door, wait outside for a few moments, walk slowly around to the front of the theater, enter again, and—this time—be very sure that I was seen by the man in the office. Then, in going down to the dressing room again, I could bolt that door, on the inside, as it had been."

Jim's eyes looked dark and shining. The confused voices of sheriff and men were coming closer.

Jim said, whispering: "*Adelaide.*"

"No one else entered after eight o'clock. If she had had time to plan, she wouldn't have made up Cholster. But she was frantic, excited, obliged to snatch at defense. This time she snatched at an alibi. Dickenson discovered the murder only a moment or two after her arrival. But it was her second arrival. He really hadn't seen her at first. He was too intent on the girl in Springfield probably."

"But the motive?"

"Remember Cholster controlled her money and thus actually controlled her. He was tyrannical and violent-tempered. It seemed to me that her sobs were more frightened petulance than sorrow. And that she was much more concerned about Dickenson than anything else. That's what I meant and what Jane meant when she replied. Probably Dickenson talked marriage: Cholster objected; refused to give Adelaide money that was rightfully her own; and Dickenson—I don't suppose he wanted her without money."

"And then she heard the telephone conversation——"

"Yes," said Susan soberly. "She entered the theater and heard that. And jealousy—rage—the fury of a woman who sees the only thing she wants denied her (a vain woman, clutching at youth)—all of it swept to a climax. She walked up to the stage and saw Cholster lying there asleep. And *at the same instant* saw a weapon for her vengeance and for her release hanging there over his head."

"It's her lipstick?"

"Yes. It was in her coat pocket; that's why she sent for her coat. Jane uses none. Adelaide does, and you can see a smear of it on her lips now. It's called claret—a rather soft crimson. Any woman would note the exact shade. And Tom Remy saw it, too. He was looking in Cholster's make-up box to see if there was a stick of lip paste of that shade of soft crimson. And without the odor of grease paints. But then," said Susan slowly, "perhaps they all knew in their hearts who did it—and why. Jane admitted that. And—for proof there are fingerprints on the bolt of the stage door where Adelaide had to touch it."

The sheriff reached the footlights and stopped.

Without looking Susan could see the group at the other side of the stage.

"So," said the sheriff, "there's a murder here."

Jim's hand touched Susan's shoulder.

"The car's outside at the corner where we left it. Go on and wait for me there."

### The Man Who Was Missing

SUSAN DARE WAITED in the dusk. Above her into the night rose the dim, dark outline of Notre Dame. The heavy doors behind her slowly opened now and then, and closed, as an occasional figure went in or out of the church. Mariette, thought Susan, ought to come soon. Perhaps she herself was a little early at their meeting place, for she hadn't known exactly how to find the French quarter. She hadn't, in fact, known that there was a French quarter in all Chicago.

Yet she hadn't been surprised when Mariette Berne told her that, until times were better, she was living there. She would, of course, have sought her own people. Susan wondered if she would recognize the girl. It had been so long since Susan had been taken in frilly white dresses and huge hair-ribbons to Monsieur Berne's dancing school. Mariette Berne had been then a tiny, dark-eyed wisp of a child; dancing, said the elders approvingly, like a fairy. And now years had passed, and Monsieur Berne's dancing school was no more, and tiny Mariette Berne had grown up and had become a ballet dancer and had telephoned to Susan out of that fragrant past.

If it hadn't been for that past, if the girl's voice hadn't been so soft and appealing, if she hadn't—— Come, now, Susan admonished Susan, admit the truth! It's not sentiment that's brought you here. And it's not because a probably fourth-rate artist has taken it into his head to disappear and that he was engaged to marry little Mariette Berne. It's because of the soap on the shaving brush.

A woman came swiftly from the dusk and approached the door of the church. She was tall and slender and, as there was a light above the door, Susan caught an instant's glimpse of a singularly regular face and carefully arranged dark hair. There was something about her—her hat, perhaps, or the sleek lines of her thin light gown— that was not what Susan would have expected to see just there. But at the moment she was only concerned with the fact that the woman could not be Mariette Berne, for she did not hesitate at sight of Susan but went rather hurriedly into the church, and the door closed behind her.

It was terrifically hot. Susan shifted the thin

white coat on her arm and was thankful she had worn the thinnest, coolest tailored white silk her summer wardrobe included.

She wished that Mariette would come. And just then she came, emerging from the twilight.

Susan recognized her at once. Her great, soft dark eyes had changed only to hold sorrow. Her hair made a dark cloud for her heart-shaped face, which with maturity had grown beautiful. Her hand met and clung to Susan's.

"Oh, Miss Dare—you will do it, then? You will find André?"

"I'll try," said Susan, wishing the girl's eyes were not so terribly beseeching. "I'll try. But I may not succeed."

"Oh, but you will," cried the girl with soft earnestness. "I know about you. I've read your books—you can solve *any* mystery."

"Look here, my dear," said Susan gently. "Are you sure that you want to know? Can you face it if——"

"If—he's dead, you mean?" breathed the girl. Her hands clasped and unclasped, but there was suddenly a clear, firm strength about her mouth. "I must know," she said in a whisper. "Whatever it is—*I must know.*"

It wasn't what Susan had meant. A voluntary disappearance on the part of the artist had been in her mind.

"You see," added Mariette quite simply, "he would let me know—if he could. If he were alive he would let me know."

After a moment Susan leaned over toward the small dressing case she had brought. "You've told Madame Touseau that you were bringing me?" she asked.

"Yes," said Mariette. "There is a room next to mine. I told her you were a friend of mine. Out of a job." They walked down the steps and off into the mysterious dusk. "But Madame," said Mariette doubtfully, "is very keen."

"Let me see if I have things straight. Madame Touseau owns the house where you live?"

"Yes. There are several roomers. She calls us guests. We have meals there, too, and it is very good cooking. Everything is very clean, and doesn't cost much."

"How many people live there?"

"There's me. And André had a studio in the top floor—the attic. Then there are now, only Mr. Kinder, and Louis Malmin. The maid-of-all-work, Agnes, sleeps out."

"Tell me again," said Susan, "just what happened."

"Well—first you must understand that Madame is very sharp. Nothing at all happens in the house that she does not discover one way or another. I mean, when she says the doors were bolted for the night *after* the guests were all inside the house, and that André did not go out again before the doors were bolted, then that is right. Of course, now, she says that she is not sure. But the doors were bolted on the inside the next morning. I know that."

"Windows?" suggested Susan.

"I don't think so," said Mariette. "His windows are very high, you know, with a straight drop to the street. And in these streets it is well to keep houses locked. That night—that was Wednesday night, two nights ago—André said good-night to me there in the corridor. I watched him walk up the stairs to his studio in the attic. At the door he turned and waved at me, as he always does. And—that was the last time he was seen. He closed the door and—vanished. Simply dropped out of sight."

They walked on for a few steps in silence.

Around them, lining the narrow streets, were tall houses, their shabbiness and their smoke-stained walls hidden by the night.

When Susan spoke, her voice had lowered.

"Madame did not want you to call the police?"

"She would not permit it," said the girl slowly. "Madame—is very determined. As you will see."

Madame's changing story bothered Susan. Still, perhaps the woman had honestly not heard André's departure, and then, when it became evident that he had gone, had been obliged to admit her mistake. Yet the door had been bolted on the inside: was that a mistake—or had he gone out some other way? After all, there were windows on the first floor.

"Madame," said Mariette softly, "would be in a rage if she knew that I had told you. She says that André grew tired—of me."

"I expect he could have got out of the house some way if he had wanted to," said Susan, lost in thought.

"Perhaps," said Mariette, in a way that rejected it completely. "But there is the shaving brush, Miss Dare. A man does not put soap on a wet shaving brush and then make up his mind to disappear. And do so taking nothing at all with him. Not even his money."

"Money?"

"Not very much," said Mariette with a sigh. "It was hidden under a brick of the fireplace. I took it," she added with simplicity. "No need to let Madame find it. I will take care of it for him. There's only a little."

"Have you watched the papers?" asked Susan.

"Oh, yes. There's been nothing. No accident—no—" the girl choked and said—"no suicide. Nothing that I could think would be André."

Well, of course, a man would scarcely start to shave, be overcome with a desire to commit suicide in the middle of it, and dash away to hurl himself—where? In the river, perhaps.

And there was something strange, something indecipherable about Mariette's bald little story that caught and held Susan. It might prove to be merely a voluntary disappearance of a man who was important only to himself and to Mariette. Yet its very unimportance was perplexing. Why had he disappeared so suddenly and so completely?

"Had he any enemies?" she asked abruptly.
"Did he ever seem to have sums of money?"
"No, no. You are thinking of racketeers. It was nothing like that. André wanted only to paint."

If he had not left of his own free will, then he had been kidnaped. Or murdered. Murder was probably not unknown along that street. But what was the motive?

Quite suddenly Susan thought of Jim Byrne. But he had been out of town for a week following a difficult assignment that had to do with an extradition case then usurping newspaper space. And besides, Jim had not seen the appeal in the girl's soft dark eyes.

"But André has been gone only two nights," Susan said. "Surely you need not——" She never knew what she had intended to say, for the girl whirled suddenly toward her. Her white face and dark eyes looked tragic in the dusk.

"I am afraid," said the girl tensely. "There is something wrong about the house. Something terribly wrong. Something—— Here is the house, Miss Dare."

She turned, and Susan looked up at the darkly looming house above them and was conscious of a wish that Jim had returned. Well, she could leave if she wanted to. There was nothing at all to keep her there.

A heavy door, stained with many years of Chicago's smoke, closed behind them, and Susan blinked in the mellow light of a spacious and somewhat elegant entrance hall. The house had been evidently one of the half circle about Chicago of one-time beautiful residences that gave way gradually to the encroachments of warehouses and factories and the steady wave of foreign breadwinners.

Then Mariette was leading her to the wide doorway and into a long crowded living room—crowded with furniture, crowded with plants in pots, crowded with embroidered and laced cushions and footstools and table covers.

There were two people in the room. A woman of perhaps fifty sat under a light, with her sleek, dark hair bent over something like a cushion on her lap. Not far from her a man at a table played some kind of card game.

"Madame," said Mariette, "it is my friend, Miss Dare."

Madame turned, and the light fell strongly upon her. She was dark and heavy and scrupulously neat. Her features were coarse and strong and swarthy. Her eyes were very black, she had a faint mustache across her upper lip, and there were two black marks like warts on one lower eyelid which gave her an extremely sinister look.

She looked Susan up and down. Clearly Madame Touseau's roomers had to pass some test and standard hidden away back in Madame Touseau's Gallic mind. Clearly, too, there was something about Susan which did not altogether please Madame Touseau.

She said something in quick French to Mariette, and Susan caught only Mariette's reply, which was something about a department store and seemed to reassure Madame.

She smiled, disclosing strong yellow teeth.

"You may have one of my rooms," she said. "I'll show you at once. A friend of Mariette's ——" She did not finish, and Susan felt that Mariette had vouched for her respectability. The man at the table flipped the cards together with a sigh.

Madame was rolling up intricate white threads. She was an expert lace-maker, for her strong broad hands were inconceivably quick and delicate in their touch. The tiny wooden bobbins clicked faintly against each other as she put down the cushion upon which she worked and which held, firmly pinned, the lace she was making.

"Is it as hot outdoors as it is inside?" said the man at the table, turning to watch and rippling the cards idly.

"Worse," said Mariette. "Miss Dare, this is Mr. Kinder."

Kinder rose and bowed. He was a man of somewhat uncertain age, with a thin face and shoulders and a surprising thickness of body upon long thin legs. His hair was black and he wore a straggly beard, black also. His eyes looked tired and wearily sharp. A small muscle near his mouth twitched as he said something polite to Susan.

Madame said abruptly: "Will you come with me, Miss Dare? I must ask you to sign my guest register. This is not the hotel nor the rooming house, but one is obliged to follow the letter of the law, nevertheless."

She snapped on the light above a long blotter-covered table in the hall, and pulled forward a small ledger.

"Your name, please, and former address. And your occupation. Here is a pen."

Susan sat down slowly in the chair Madame pulled forward and took the pen. Madame was taking no chances—yet perhaps the register was demanded by law and not, as it looked, a ruse to protect herself against unwelcome guests.

Susan looked at the names written on the page Madame placed before her. Looked, and her eyes became thoughtful.

Mariette had not been mistaken then. There was something wrong about the house.

Aware of Madame's brooding regard, Susan slowly wrote her name and address in the space below Louis Malmin. Taking advantage of Mariette's statement that she was out of a job, she left the occupation unnamed.

Madame read it and led the way upstairs.

The room to which she showed Susan was terrifically hot and airless but scrupulously clean. Susan opened the windows as soon as Madame had gone.

The night was hot and still, too, with not a breath of air moving. Away off somewhere she could hear the faint rush and clangor of an elevated train, muffled by heat and distance.

Above her was the third-floor studio from which André Cavalliere had so curiously vanished. Tomorrow she would examine it at her leisure.

Mariette, coming quietly to the door, told her definitely of the arrangement of the rooms which Madame had let to her guests. Mariette's own room was beside Susan's, with a vacant room beyond that. Across the back of the house was another vacant room.

"Madame, herself," said Mariette, "has the large room at the front of the house, at the head of the stairs. Across the hall is Mr. Kinder's room: it is the largest and best room, and he pays more than the rest of us. Then beside his room is that of Louis."

"Louis Malmin, is it?"

"Yes. Louis Malmin. An importer of oriental things: he is here for the Century of Progress."

"How long has he been here?"

"Nearly two years. He knows André. André did some silhouettes for him. But they are on good terms."

"Who is Kinder?"

"He was here when I came two years ago. He is a retired salesman. He is not in good health."

"Does he know André?"

"Oh, yes. We are all well acquainted. Madame calls us her family."

Susan had not been strongly impressed with a sense of the sincerity of Madame's sentiment. Still, a tiger could purr for its food and hide the unsheathing of its claws. "It's late," said Susan. "We'll talk in the morning."

But after Mariette had gone, she sat at the window for a long time. Madame, Mariette, Kinder, and Louis Malmin. André Cavalliere who had vanished in that hot, silent house.

Two nights ago, when André Cavalliere had gone to his attic studio and vanished, there had been only four others in the house. Had one of them had something to do with that disappearance?

In the silence of the night it seemed possible.

Down the hall Madame was waiting like a sleeping tiger behind her closed door. Susan felt altogether sure that Madame would know of any sound or movement on the stairway or along the the hall. If André Cavalliere had gone out that night, Madame would have known of it. But if he had not gone out, what had happened to him?

It was not a pleasant thought, and it haunted Susan through a long and stifling night.

Morning dawned; the air was still hot and misty, and it was an effort to breathe.

While the others were at breakfast in the dining room downstairs Mariette took Susan up to the third floor.

"I took the key," she said, unlocking the low door that led directly from the stairway into the wide, long room which extended, except where it had been walled up under the eaves, over the entire space of the house. The walls and low ceiling, which followed in outline the peaked roof, had been plastered and were hung with a variety of paintings.

At one end was a sort of kitchen, with a small gas plate and a table and some shelves. Along one side and behind a screen was a couch and a mirror and dressing table.

"There," said Mariette, pointing, and Susan bent to look closely at the small congregation of shaving tools—the shaving brush had dried, but little white ribbons of soap clung to it as if they had just been squeezed out of the tube of shaving soap that lay beside it, except that they too had dried. A safety razor was there, also.

It was, of course, exactly what Mariette had already described to her, but as she looked at the bits of white soap and the unused razor blade, Susan found herself convinced: André Cavalliere had not intended to disappear. That much, at least, was certain.

"Have you found something?"

"No more than you told me," said Susan. "Where was the money hidden?"

Mariette led the way quickly to the fireplace at the front of the room. The brick was loose, and it was evident—or would have been evident to a searcher—that it was loose. So probably the money had had nothing to do with the thing. Except to indicate again that André Cavalliere had not intended to disappear.

Susan looked thoughtfully about the room. It was evidently here that he had worked and lounged. There were shabby but comfortable-looking chairs. Easels. A paint-smeared table. Ash trays. A small rug or two, very thin and worn. Queer that the rugs were arranged with so little regard for need or symmetry. One was flung crookedly before the fireplace. One was straight enough below a chair, but the chair had been placed so that it stood at an awkward angle to the rest of the room.

Susan walked over to the chair.

Odd that the chair was placed so carefully in the very center of the rug. Odd——

Someone was coming up the attic stairs.

Madame opened the door; her dark eyes swept keenly over Susan and Mariette.

"So Mariette has been telling you her troubles," she said harshly. "Mariette is a silly girl. The young man has gone. Yes. But it is not for Mariette to find him. He will return if he so desires. Your breakfast," said Madame firmly, "is waiting."

Madame too possessed a key to the studio room, and she locked the door firmly behind them. Susan saw Mariette's slender hand close upon her own key.

And it was as they reached the second floor again that the incident occurred that was, then, so trivial.

And that was the breakfast tray, laden with soiled dishes and a crumpled napkin, which stood upon the bottom step. Madame halted as she saw it, then swept forward, took it up in her wide hands, and looked at Susan and Mariette.

"Mr. Malmin," she said, "had breakfast in his own room this morning. Agnes is very careless. She ought not to have put the tray on the steps."

She turned, and her thin black dress billowed out after her as she went down the steps to the first floor.

As they followed, Susan put out her hand silently toward Mariette who, understanding, gave her the key to the studio.

Madame poured coffee for them and rustled away.

When, an hour later, Susan went to her room again, Madame was sitting in her own room with the door wide open and herself in such a position as to command a view of the entire length of the corridor and the entrance to the narrow third-floor stairway. Susan opened her door, ostensibly to catch any stirring of cool air, and took up a book, and thus entered upon a prolonged and silent duel with the black-eyed Frenchwoman. Mariette came nervously into the corridor now and then, looked at Susan and at Madame, and vanished again.

John Kinder's door remained closed. But once another man, short and stocky and supple, with a dark, hawk-like face, emerged from the room directly opposite Susan's, gave her a quick, keen look, and went down the stairway.

That was, of course, the man Mariette had called Louis Malmin. He looked, Susan was bound to admit, fully capable of accomplishing all the crimes in the Decalogue, alone and unaided. But there was nothing to link him with André. Nothing, indeed, so far, to link André with any of them except Mariette. Unless Madame's vigilance was a clue to—well, to what?

It was late in the afternoon when Susan contrived an errand to take Madame's attention. Although it was actually Mariette who induced the Frenchwoman to examine the money she had taken from André's room. They were downstairs in the living room by that time, and Madame was still vigilant.

"Money!" said Madame. "You took money from his room! How much?"

"I—haven't counted it," said Mariette with unexpected guile. "I thought it was safer with me. Do you want to look at it?"

Madame looked at Susan and looked at Mariette. It was, however, Susan thought, the only bait to which she would have risen.

"Perhaps I'd better see it," she said. "If

André Cavalliere does not return, I shall be obliged to claim this money. He owes me—you understand?"

Quietly Susan followed them. When she heard Mariette close the door to her room she hurried along the corridor and, at last, up the steps to the third floor again.

She was always glad that Mariette had not been with her when she moved the chair and looked under the rug.

For under the rug, plain against the old pine floor was a queer, irregular mark. It was not blood—but blood had been there and had been recently and thoroughly washed. Susan sat back on her heels and looked at that mark.

The conclusion, of course, was obvious.

Madame's vigilance took on a new and sinister meaning. That meant, then, that she knew something of the thing that had happened here.

Susan rose.

It did not take long to look carefully over the entire studio, for André Cavalliere had not been widely possessed of this world's goods. Indeed, the only thing of interest Susan found was that André had smoked many cigarettes since the ash trays had been emptied; and that he had sketched everybody in the house in every possible pose.

Susan glanced rapidly through the portfolio crammed with sketches that lay on the broad table. There was Madame—Madame in workaday black; Madame's glossy head bent over her lace; Madame facing her, with lids drooped over her dark eyes. There were sketches of John Kinder, his beard waggish and shaven and church-wardenish in turns. Sketches of Louis Malmin—one apparently a joke on the part of the artist, in which Louis Malmin appeared with a handkerchief tied round his head, huge rings in his ears, a wide knife between his white teeth, and something that was not a joke looking out of his eyes. There were sketches of a woman of great beauty of feature who looked vaguely familiar to Susan. There were sketches of Mariette—many of them. Susan closed the portfolio and put it under her arm.

She must hurry. Mariette could not keep Madame counting money forever.

She paused to replace the rug and the chair. Who had placed them there? Who had scrubbed in cold water that stain below until it was lighter than all the rest of the floor? Who—she bent over and took in her fingers a small object that lay wedged into the cushions of the chair so that only its blunt end had showed, and she stood there a moment, turning it in her fingers slowly. It was a small wooden bobbin. The kind that is used in making lace.

She closed her hand upon it. The attic was growing rapidly darker, and the heat was becoming sultry, as it does before an electrical storm. Madame's hands, strong and broad, making lace assiduously. Madame's hands carrying that breakfast tray. Madame's hands scrubbing out the stain on the floor. She was somehow sure that the Frenchwoman had done that.

Susan decided she'd had enough of the attic and started for the stairway.

The hall below was empty and rather dark. But as she went quietly along it toward her own room a door away down at the end opened, and Madame's figure was silhouetted against the light from a window in the room beyond.

That room was vacant. Why had Susan so strong an impression that there was someone in the room? Was it something about the fleeting glimpse of a turn of Madame's head—a feeling that words had been quickly hushed?

At first Susan thought that, in the sudden dusk of the narrow corridor, Madame did not see her. But she opened her own door and a soft shaft of greenish light from the window beyond struck her face and she saw that black-clad figure hesitate.

There was a small bolt on the door, and Susan fastened it against unexpected interruption before she opened the portfolio and spread the sketches in a wide circle around her on the floor.

Slowly she arranged them so that all the sketches of one person were in a group, and she studied, fascinated, the results of that arrangement.

She had known these people always—she had known those varying expressions familiarly and long. Thus Madame looked when she was pleased; purring and complacent because a new lodger was prompt in paying. So Madame looked when intent on her lace-making. So when she was in festive mood. Thus when she was angry.

Louis Malmin in as many moods; studying them, there was one thing always predominant in the hawk-like, piratical face with its small dark eyes that were just a bit too close set, and that was acquisitiveness. Greed. A subordination of everything else in life to an overmastering need for gain.

Yes, perhaps André Cavalliere's only forte lay in a strange flair for character divination— so that, with one stroke of a pencil, he could place driving greed in Louis Malmin's eyes.

John Kinder, with time at his disposal, had posed exhaustively. Here he was in a dozen aspects, and Susan lingered over each. Here was Mariette, too: Susan looked at those sketches for a long time, and when she had finished was convinced of one thing at least, and that was that the artist had loved Mariette. He had not of his own volition left her. But then she had known that already. Poor little Mariette.

It was so dark when Susan pulled herself from a reverie into which she had plunged and turned to the last group of pictures that she had to reach up and turn on the single electric globe that hung from the ceiling in order to see the face of the unknown woman. There were only two poses of her, and as the bright light poured garishly down upon it, Susan remembered where she had seen that face with its almost too perfect regularity of feature.

It was certainly that of the woman who **had**

emerged so swiftly from the dusk the previous night while Susan was waiting for Mariette; the woman who had slipped quickly up the steps, fleetingly under the light and into the church of Notre Dame.

Susan frowned and pushed back her soft light hair. Did that entirely account for the familiarity of that perfectly regular face? And if it was a face she had seen somewhere and frequently, whose was it?

She sighed and wished the storm would blow over, and fell to studying the pictures again. She lingered very long over one sketch.

Moments passed while the sky slowly darkened and the hot still house awaited the storm. And by the time Mariette knocked timidly at the door, Susan knew things that she had not known before.

The sound of the knock roused her from a queer, rather terrifying thought that André Cavalliere had left behind him what was, in effect, a record of his death.

For he had been murdered. Susan was sure of that.

What should she do?

To inform the police would be, just then, futile. She could say: I think this man was murdered because there's a mark on the floor of his studio that has recently been scrubbed and which I think was blood. Because he has disappeared. Because his sketch portfolio holds certain faces in certain poses. They would say and rightly: Where is the body?

If she knew only a little more—and that little was something that had nothing to do with the blind, fumbling search into currents of thought and feeling around her that was at once Susan's strength and Susan's weakness. She smiled a little wryly. If Jim had been there it would have helped. Without him she must herself confirm instinct—if that was what it was—with reason. With clues. With definite evidence.

"Come in," she said to Mariette's knock, and then remembered the door was bolted and scrambled to her feet to open it.

As Mariette entered, pale as a ghost in her limp white dress, Susan scooped up the sketches, permitting one of the woman of Notre Dame to remain on top.

"Do you know this woman?" she asked Mariette directly.

"No," said Mariette. "But it's one of André's sketches."

"You've never seen her?"

"N-no. That is, there's something vaguely familiar about her. But I'm sure I don't know her. And I never saw this sketch before."

"Has there been any time since you knew André when this woman could have been in the house without your knowing it?"

"Oh, yes. I was on tour for six weeks, last fall. She could have been here then. Louis Malmin was gone at that time, too, on a business trip. And—yes, I remember, that was the time when Mr. Kinder was gone, too. A vacation trip, he said, of about a week. But if she was here then— this woman, I mean—André didn't tell me. You don't mean—you don't think he's gone with her?" Her dark eyes sought Susan beseechingly.

"No," said Susan gently. "He has not gone with her. Has Madame Touseau any family? Any children or—any relatives at all? Or even any intimate friends?"

Mariette shook her head.

"No. Except that I believe she has a niece somewhere in California. But I've never seen her. And Madame keeps very much to herself. She often says her—well, she calls us all guests, you know—are her only family." Mariette hesitated. "I'm afraid," she said, "that Madame knows why you are here. She asked me—oh, a great many questions. She—" Mariette shivered a little in that hot, still room—"*she watches us so.*"

Susan delved into confused thoughts and went back for something, some word that had been spoken, that must be explored.

And she must herself this time, without Jim's help, confirm with hard fact the findings of the queer divining rod of her own consciousness. Of the blind little tentacles of something that was so dangerously like intuition and yet was not quite that either.

The silence lay as heavy as the leaves outside.

Then Susan said:

"Mariette—I want you to go out and get me some things, and I don't want Madame to see them when you return."

She paused, glancing at the open transom. Then she crossed to the window and examined the old-fashioned shade and the light rod that held the hem of it flat and straight.

"Bring me," said Susan Dare, "all the movie magazines you can find. And a mirror—a shaving mirror will do, but I'd rather have one of those small make-up mirrors: you've seen them. They have a little standard and are about six inches in diameter. And at dinner tonight when everyone is seated at the table I want you to tell Madame that you are going to inform the police of André's disappearance. Make it emphatic. And again, when I talk of André, follow my lead. Agree with me."

"Yes," said Mariette and was gone.

Susan hid the sketches and opened her door. Madame's door was closed. Probably she had taken up her observation post in the drawing room downstairs. Susan looked about her room, discovered a small push-button bell, and rang it.

Her little plan, however, failed. Either the bell was disconnected or Agnes, the somewhat mysterious servant, was busy in the kitchen. Susan rang several times, but there was still no answer.

Well, the matter of Agnes could wait.

But she must know who was in that supposedly vacant room. Or rather who was not in the room.

But again she failed. For though she managed to approach the closed door to the room at the back of the house without, so far as she knew, having been seen, there was no sound from within. She listened, bending her head to the blank dark panels and holding her breath. But there was no sound at all on the other side of that door. She wanted to knock; she wanted to open the door. But something about the silence and the darkness of the place held her silent, too, and not too certain of herself. After all, a man had been murdered in that house—murdered deliberately and in cold blood. She was as certain of that as she was ever in her whole life certain of anything.

And the murder had been skillfully, carefully concealed. So skillfully and so carefully that there remained no evidence at all to show that it had been done. No evidence but the thin brown mark around that clean spot under the rug. No evidence but the sketches in André Cavalliere's portfolio.

But the murderer had made one mistake.

And that night, if Susan's conclusions were right, there would be an attempt to make that mistake right.

And what could she do then? She would need help—and she must be sure.

There was still no rustle of motion within that room. Susan went quietly back to her own room, took her hat and, boldly this time, went through the hall toward the front and down the stairs.

Madame, bent over her lace, looked up. John Kinder let a card fall from his hand and looked up also.

"I'm going out a bit," said Susan. "If Mariette asks for me, won't you tell her I've gone for a little walk?"

Madame's black eyes plunged across the dusk into Susan's.

"The door," said Madame calmly, "is locked. And I have the key. Mariette has just gone out for a little walk, too. But I shouldn't advise Miss Dare to go. Because," said Madame Touseau slowly, "it is about to storm. Mademoiselle would not like to be caught in a storm."

Susan gripped the stair railing. Absurd that her heart had leaped so suddenly to pound in her throat.

She shot a glance at John Kinder. But he had gone placidly back to his card game as if altogether unaware of the threat in Madame's heavy voice.

Susan left the stairway, but Madame reached the door first. Her thick body was an indomitable barrier.

"That gown," said the Frenchwoman, "is too beautiful—too expensive to permit to be ruined. Me, I know the handsome dressmaking. I am not one to be deceived about that—that," she repeated slowly, "or other things. I do not believe Miss Dare wishes the walk in the rain. No."

It was then an open threat. Yet the woman could not keep her jailed for long in that house. She dared not.

Dared not? There was that other thing she had dared.

Susan thought swiftly. It was time for which the woman was playing. She must need time—otherwise her opposition would have taken an entirely different line. Susan restrained a desire to combat the woman openly; for an instant the thought of physical struggle over the key, a mad desire to escape, to be gone from that fetid, silent house with the stain of blood overhead, clutched at Susan as hysteria would clutch.

But the Frenchwoman was stronger. And there was Kinder. And behind Susan quite suddenly on the steps another voice spoke. The words, however, were altogether commonplace.

"Madame Touseau," said Louis Malmin quietly, "may I have dinner a little early tonight?"

As if a puzzle had given itself a jerk so that pieces which had been distorted and confused fell suddenly into a regular and ordinary pattern, so, all at once the queer little scene changed and became regular and ordinary. Susan's breath began to come freely. Madame's dark face was smooth and efficient as she spoke calmly to Louis Malmin.

She had merely advised Susan not to go out in the rain. That was all.

"Will you unlock the door, Madame Touseau?" said Susan. "I wish to go out before the rain comes."

Would the woman boldly refuse?

But her dark eyes met Susan's and glowed. Then she smiled and said:

"But certainly, if one wishes." She turned and opened the door. "However—when the storm comes it will be bad."

Susan was conscious of Kinder's face turned inquiringly toward her; of Louis Malmin's presence there on the stairway behind her. But the door to the street stood open, and Susan walked past Madame and out upon the steps.

A string of shops ought to be found a street or two beyond, for Susan remembered vaguely a patch of radiance off toward her right as she and Mariette had walked from the church the night before. She turned in that direction.

Her easy victory was perplexing; it led Susan to doubt her own conclusions. For it was as if Madame had warned her merely to go no further but had scorned, smilingly, any notion that Susan was already in possession of a fact that might be dangerous.

It became clearer to Susan that the little episode had been merely a warning on Madame Touseau's part. Madame, then, was very sure of herself. But she did not know that Susan had seen the sketches. She did not know that one of her own wooden bobbins was at that moment in Susan's white handbag. She did not know that Susan had seen the woman on the church steps.

Yet perhaps the entire fabric of reasoning

that Susan had built up was wrong. Perhaps she had missed some salient and pivotal fact.

Few corners are without drugstores and the corner upon which Susan emerged was no exception. It was small and crowded at the soda fountain where perspiring and frenzied clerks dealt out tall, iced glasses. Susan supplied herself with nickels and went to the little row of mahogany-stained telephone booths at the back.

The telephone number of the *Record* is famous in Chicago. Susan called it and waited. Jim had been out of town yesterday, of course; but that didn't mean that he was not in town today. If he had not returned, she didn't know exactly what to do next; it would be best, perhaps, simply to wait. But she wasn't sure that she dared wait.

It was terrifically hot in the little booth. A faraway voice said it was the *Record* and referred her to another voice which hesitated and then to Susan's immense relief, turned and called distantly: "Hey, Jim!"

"Hello—hello——"

It was Jim Byrne.

"Jim," said Susan in a small voice, "oh, Jim, I'm so glad you are here."

"Oh, hello, Sue. What's the matter?"

"I don't know. I don't know, but I think it's murder——"

"My God!" said Jim. "In this heat!"

"And I think I know who did it."

"*Where are you? Where's the body?*"

"I'm at Sibley and Loomis——"

"What?" shouted Jim.

"At Sibley and Loomis," repeated Susan firmly. "In a drugstore in a booth."

Then Jim said: "You sound scared. Stay there where you are. I'll be there in—oh, ten minutes. 'Bye."

Susan sat down at a table. "Two tall lemonades," she said to the white-aproned boy who approached. "With lots of ice."

"Two?" he said, eyeing Susan as if measuring her capacity.

Jim bettered his promise by three minutes.

"Angel," he said looking at the frosted glass, "is that for me?"

"Drink it," said Susan. "And don't ask me questions till I've finished. Jim, is there anyone who might be in hiding there at Madame Touseau's? That is a rooming house in the French quarter. Someone a great deal in the public eye; someone who would want to escape attention?"

He grinned.

"A lot of people, my Susan. The bird I've been trying to locate for one." He took a long swallow and added: "But everybody says he's got out of the country. Best for his health. You've read about the Anton Burgess disclosures. As long as he can stay out of sight a whole lot of fellows here in Chicago are that much better off. There's an embezzlement charge."

Susan frowned.

"Yes, I read that. Jim, can you come back there with me? You see, I've got some sketches that I want to show you. The main facts of the thing are simple. A man by the name of André Cavalliere, an artist, engaged to marry little Mariette Berne——"

"Berne," said Jim. "That little ballet dancer?"

"Yes. He—well, he just vanished. And I think he's murdered."

"Why?"

"Because," said Susan, "there's blood on the attic floor. And it's been washed."

Jim gave her a long look. Then he beckoned to the boy. "Two more drinks," he said. "Whose blood, Susan?"

"I want you to see the sketches," she said obliquely. "I want to know if you see in them what I see." She frowned again. "Burgess," she said thoughtfully. "Yes, that might be right." Jim put down his glass.

"Look here, Susan," he said earnestly, "if you've stumbled over Anton Burgess, lead me there, Miss Santa Claus. Every paper in the United States has been trying to find him for nearly two years."

Susan shook her head. "Are you sure you would recognize him if you saw him?"

"Yes," he said soberly. "I believe so—you're keeping something back, Susan. What is it?"

She shook her head again. "I want you to see it for yourself," she said. "I may be wrong."

He stared at her over the empty glasses. His blue eyes were thoughtful; his irregular but agreeable features were intent.

"All right," he said. "Are we apt to need reinforcements?"

"Police? No. It's a case for your Irish tongue,

Jim. I think," said Susan slowly, "that we've got a lever that you can work."

He flipped the coins to the weary boy. They emerged upon a heat-stricken street. They turned toward Notre Dame.

"I'd forgotten there was a French quarter," said Jim. "What a place for anyone to hide! A forgotten section in the middle of a great city. Hedged in completely with little foreign worlds. Tell me all, Sue."

"Well," said Susan cautiously, "I've made a little plan. It's not much. But it may work. I sent Mariette for some movie magazines. And a small mirror."

"The mirror," said Jim, "suggests a periscope. But I'll be damned if I know what you want movie magazines for. And how are you going to get me in this place? Tell them you've picked up a boy-friend?"

"I don't know," said Susan, eyeing him doubtfully. "I don't think even money would persuade Madame to take another lodger just now. Especially a suspiciously well-tailored one arriving promptly upon my return. I believe the simplest way will be best—that is, for me to let you in while the others are at dinner."

It was quite simple. The house was very much darker than the street and though a light burned in the drawing room there was no one to see Jim cross the hall. With the knowledge that Jim was upstairs, Susan felt more certain of herself.

Susan was never to forget the dinner—her first and last dinner—in Madame Touseau's house. She was always to remember the narrow room with its brown walls, its mirrored built-in sideboard, and its heavy hanging center light. There was unexpectedly good linen and soup, and Madame, erect, with her black hair and eyes gleaming, presided quite as if they were in truth her guests. Louis Malmin was directly opposite Susan. John Kinder ate sparingly of what appeared to be a vegetable diet and said very little. As Susan appeared, Mariette uttered a little gasp of relief which she tried to cover by saying something about the storm.

A window had been opened, and now and then a hot breath of air swept the lace curtain inward and then sucked it back against the screen. Wasn't that an indication of a cyclonic area? thought Susan, accepting chicken gumbo and her first glimpse of the servant, Agnes, at the same time. Agnes was a plain, fat little woman, about as mysterious as a post, and she retired immediately to the kitchen.

Mariette lifted her dark eyes and looked straight at Madame Touseau.

"I think I'd better tell you," she said, "that I am going to call the police tomorrow morning."

Madame's face darkened, and she shot a swift suspicious glance at Susan.

"You mean to investigate the departure of André?"

"Exactly," said Mariette with unaccustomed decision.

Madame's broad hands fingered the silver beside her plate.

John Kinder paused with a forkful of lettuce in the air to look in a mildly reproving manner at Mariette, and Louis Malmin ate steadily.

"There are some sketches that André made," said Susan. "They are very interesting sketches. So interesting that we thought the police might be able to——" She stopped herself abruptly, as if she had said more than she had intended to say.

There was a little silence.

Then Madame said:

"Sketches. What kind of sketches?"

"Oh, nothing much. Just little bits of—everyday things. Street scenes—people." Susan hoped she was making the right impression of flurried retraction.

"What people?" said Madame heavily.

Susan said nothing, and John Kinder let the lettuce travel to his mouth and said through it, mildly:

"Me, for one. I used to pose for André often. But I don't quite see how this young lady expects the sketches he made to help solve the problem of his disappearance. And I do think police investigation is quite uncalled for."

Mariette repeated: "I'm going to call the police." And Louis Malmin rose suddenly, spoke briefly to Madame, and left the dining room.

After that, nothing more was said of police, though John Kinder kept up a mild barrage of conversation which covered Madame's glooming silence and the general air of discomfiture that silence induced.

Under cover of the little confusion of pushing back chairs Mariette whispered to Susan: "I found the woman that André sketched in one of the movie magazines," she said. "She is Sally Gowdy."

Sally Gowdy. One of the near-stars in the movie firmament. That was why the face was so familiar.

"Go with the others," whispered Susan, and as Mariette disappeared, Agnes came to the table.

"Agnes," said Susan directly, "for how many days have you been arranging extra trays?"

Agnes blinked, hesitated, and was lost.

"Since Monday," she said. "And I don't see where Mr. Malmin puts it all. Six meals a day that makes for him! Besides the extra work!"

Thoughtfully Susan returned to the living room. Madame had taken up her lace-making again.

Mariette had waited for her, and she and Susan walked quietly toward the stairs. Over the banisters Susan saw that John Kinder was again mildly intent upon his card game. And as she paused at her own room, she caught a gleam of light from the transom above Louis Malmin's door.

"Go on to your room, Mariette," she said in a whisper. "Lock the door, and don't let anyone—anyone, mind you—in the room. Not on any pretext."

Mariette, her small face white and ghostly in the dusk, nodded and vanished.

Jim switched off a flashlight as Susan entered. She turned on the light. The sketches were again spread, but fanwise on the floor. And the movie magazines had been rummaged and tossed aside. He knew, then. And beside the door was an odd little contraption which consisted of a mirror fastened stoutly to the end of a light wood rod, obviously taken from the head of the window shade.

His eyes were black with excitement and jubilance.

"Susan," he said in a low voice, "you've got him. It's Burgess beyond all doubt. But it took an artist to penetrate the disguise. This fellow André Cavalliere was clever—too clever for his own good. Now then, what's the program? Your periscope is ready. Are the sketches the bait?"

"That," said Susan, calmly accepting Jim's immediate comprehension, "that and a threat of police in the morning. They'll do something tonight."

"They'll do something," said Jim, "right now. Better turn out your light."

Susan did so. Afterward she remembered that

as they started their queer vigil, there was a sudden roll of thunder, close at hand and reverberating threateningly in the hushed, hot room.

Jim held the improvised periscope, which worked remarkably well, and Susan stood beside him, her eyes glued to the small reflection of the head of the stairs and a patch of intervening corridor.

"I think," said Jim in a whisper, "that I've got the main points. But there are some completely mysterious gaps. For instance, Sally Gowdy——"

"Sh-h——" breathed Susan. "You'll see, soon. There's Madame——"

It was queer to stand there in the darkness and watch Madame, a quickly moving figure with a white face, pause at the head of the stairs, look swiftly about her, and then glide directly toward them. Jim turned the mirror carefully so they could catch a glimpse of the back of the hall in time to see Madame disappear into the supposedly vacant room at its end.

There was another short wait. Very short. For the storm in all its pent-up fury swooped furiously upon the house with wind and rain and wild lightning that lit the small room eerily and then was gone.

And probably the tumult and frenzy of sound outside induced the murderer of André Cavalliere to do what must be done under cover of all that turmoil. A door along the hall opened. And a figure slipped quietly toward the attic stairway.

The mirror jerked to follow it, and Susan put her hand on Jim's arm. "Wait," she whispered. "Not yet. Wait——"

Jim would have remonstrated but she clutched his arm tighter, and he waited.

But, of course, Jim didn't know that she had no proof. That the figure that had slipped up those attic stairs must be trapped in another way.

Susan never knew how much longer they waited. The figure that had gone to the studio did not return. But finally the door at the end of the hall must have opened, for all at once there was a woman in the mirror—a woman who now crept silently along the corridor.

Susan's fingers were tight on the hard muscle of Jim's forearm.

"Now!" she said and the little mirrored picture vanished as Jim flung open the door.

The woman stopped and screamed and put her hands over her face. Then Madame Touseau was there, too.

Susan saw the glint of a revolver suddenly in Jim's hand, and the sight was inexpressibly comforting.

Madame cried: "What is the meaning of this? Who is the man? What——" She had grasped the meaning of it at once and was glaring at Susan. "You did this?" she panted.

And Jim's hand wavered suddenly on the revolver as the woman in the corridor lifted her head. "My God," he said, "it's Sally Gowdy herself!" He whirled toward Susan. "Where's Burgess?"

"Burgess," said Susan rapidly, "is upstairs in the attic, looking for the sketches. But I'm sure Madame Touseau would rather confess what she knows of the murder of André Cavalliere than have Miss Gowdy involved in a murder investigation. If you confess, Madame, merely to what you know, Miss Gowdy will be permitted to leave before the police come. You see," she said to Jim, "Miss Gowdy is Madame's niece. But, probably for publicity's sake, she does not want it known that this is her home. She arrived for a secret visit two days before the murder occurred. Madame tried to conceal the murder in order to keep Miss Gowdy out of it. It was most unfortunate that she was secretly in the house at the time. It would be still more unfortunate if the police investigation discovered her. So Madame undertook to keep them away. I am sure," said Susan, meaning the opposite, "that Madame would not have taken money from Anton Burgess for her silence."

"I don't know what you are talking about," said Madame. Her face and lips were ashen. Sally Gowdy looked up. Her beautifully regular face was stricken and terrified. Her voice that had thrilled thousands was trembling and harsh.

"Oh, tell them, tell them," she moaned. "You didn't help kill him. They can't do anything to you. And I've got to get away before the police come."

Madame's fixed dark eyes did not flicker. She said grimly: "Isn't there a thing called being an accessory after the fact?"

"There is," said Jim. "But we already know that you concealed the murder. You may as well tell it all."

"Murder——" Mariette was among them

suddenly and stood swaying, her eyes wide and piteous. "He's—dead, then——"

Madame's lips were tight.

"He's dead, you little fool," she said. "But I know only that there was blood spilled. I didn't see him dead. And I didn't help remove the body——"

"The body," whispered Mariette.

"It's in the Chicago River, I suppose," said Madame. "Burgess got rid of it that night. Does it matter?"

A crash of thunder held them silent and transfixed for a queer moment or two. Mariette's white face was blurred, and Sally Gowdy's beauty was an empty mask, and the little black spots on Madame's eyelid worked and twitched, while thunder submerged them, shaking the house, and slowly rolled away. And on its heels came a violent, sharper sound from over their heads.

Jim sprang toward the stairway, and Louis Malmin's door opened, and quite suddenly they were all surging up those narrow steps and into the attic. John Kinder was slumped over a chair. There was a table beside him, and on the table a scrap of paper. He had died instantly.

The note was confused, yet clear enough.

"You've got me," he had scrawled. "I can't find the sketches. I've known it was coming. The artist fellow recognized me and told me. But I didn't know that he had made a sketch of me as I really looked. That is what the girl meant. After he told me, there was nothing else for me to do. I used the same revolver that is here beside me. I forced the Touseau woman to conceal the fact. She was ready to do it for many reasons. But she had nothing to do with the murder. I'm ready to go. I've been hunted. I'm tired. The notes on the embezzlement case are in my trunk."

It was signed Anton Burgess, with a broken line below Burgess.

*Anton Burgess*

"Look," Susan said, "at the line below. It's broken for the downward stroke of the 'g.' That's how I knew, you see, that Kinder wasn't his real name. That a man in the house was using a name not his own. He had the same kind of line under it, but that was no reason for it to be broken, for the 'd' below which the break appears has no downward stroke. And the line extended beyond the following two letters to about the space of another letter. Thus I supposed that his real name had had seven letters with a consonant in the middle of it that went downward. The flourish of a line below his name was too strong a habit for him to break—especially when there was nothing that seemed betraying about two short lines. It told me where to look." That was later, when she was showing Jim the register and comparing the mark below the signature of John Kinder with the mark below that of Anton Burgess.

It was still later, and the storm had died, when they left the Touseau house and walked slowly toward Notre Dame.

"The sketches were the betraying evidence," said Jim thoughtfully. "Without the beard, with light hair instead of dark hair, and a youthful figure—Burgess was very much younger than he appeared as John Kinder—he was immediately recognizable as Burgess. It must have been on the artist's part an idle bit of amusement. He couldn't have dreamed what it would cost him—unless, of course, he wanted money from Burgess to keep his secret. And Burgess knew where that would lead. How did you know about Sally Gowdy?"

"I didn't," said Susan, "until I realized that the woman of Notre Dame and the woman in the sketches were the same. Therefore, that she must be here now and must have been sometime connected with the place. Then Mariette said she thought Madame had a niece in California and, of course, I thought of the movies. She was so beautiful. And it was luck that her picture was in one of the magazines. And since Agnes had been taking trays upstairs for two days *before* the murder, I knew it couldn't be André who was concealed in that supposedly vacant room. Then I realized that the movie actress and Madame would do everything possible to escape becoming involved in a murder case. I don't know why she didn't leave at once—Sally Gowdy, I mean. But, of course, I knew she would leave at once after Mariette had said she would call the police."

Notre Dame loomed darkly above them into the clear, rain-washed night. The violence of the storm had left peace and clear, wet quiet in its wake.

"Do you realize," said Jim in a hushed voice, "what a furor this news is going to make? Anton Burgess found at last—I've got to hustle, Susan! This is one time when I've got a real scoop."

"I know." She looked up at the dim outline of a cross against the sky. "Poor little Mariette," she said. "She was such a harmless little thing to be caught in such a big wheel.—All right, Jim. I'm coming."

## The Calico Dog

IT WAS NOTHING SHORT of an invitation to murder.

"You don't mean to say," Susan Dare said in a small voice, "that both of them—*both* of them are living here?"

Idabelle Lasher—Mrs. Jeremiah Lasher, that is, widow of the patent medicine emperor who died last year (resisting, it is said, his own medicine to the end with the strangest vehemence)—Idabelle Lasher turned large pale blue eyes upon Susan and sighed and said:

"Why, yes. There was nothing else to do. I can't turn my own boy out into the world."

Susan took a long breath. "Always assuming," she said, "that one of them is your own boy."

"Oh, there's no doubt about that, Miss Dare," said Idabelle Lasher simply.

"Let me see," Susan said, "if I have this straight. Your son Derek was lost twenty years ago. Recently he has returned. Rather, two of him has returned."

Mrs. Lasher was leaning forward, tears in her large pale eyes. "Miss Dare," she said, "one of them must be my son. I need him so much."

Her large blandness, her artificiality, the padded ease and softness of her life dropped away before the earnestness and honesty of that brief statement. She was all at once pathetic— no, it was on a larger scale; she was tragic in her need for her child.

"And besides," she said suddenly and with an odd naïveté, "besides, there's all that money. Thirty millions."

"*Thirty*——" began Susan and stopped. It was simply not comprehensible. Half a million, yes; even a million. But thirty millions!

"But if you can't tell yourself which of the two young men is your son, how can I? And with so much money involved——"

"That's just it," said Mrs. Lasher, leaning forward earnestly again. "I'm sure that Papa would have wanted me to be perfectly sure. The last thing he said to me was to warn me. 'Watch out for yourself, Idabelle,' he said. 'People will be after your money. Impostors.'"

"But I don't see how I can help you," Susan repeated firmly.

"You *must* help me," said Mrs. Lasher. "Christabel Frame told me about you. She said you wrote mystery stories and were the only woman who could help me, and that you were right here in Chicago."

Her handkerchief poised, she waited with childlike anxiety to see if the name of Christabel Frame had its expected weight with Susan. But it was not altogether the name of one of her most loved friends that influenced Susan. It was the childlike appeal on the part of this woman.

"How do you feel about the two claimants?" she said. "Do you feel more strongly attracted to one than to the other?"

"That's just the trouble," said Idabelle Lasher. "I like them both."

"Let me have the whole story again, won't you? Try to tell it quite definitely, just as things occurred."

Mrs. Lasher put the handkerchief away and sat up briskly.

"Well," she began. "It was like this:..." Two months ago a young man called Dixon March had called on her; he had not gone to her lawyer, he had come to see her. And he had told her a very straight story.

"You must remember something of the story—oh, but, of course, you couldn't. You're far too young. And then, too, we weren't as rich as we are now, when little Derek disappeared. He was four at the time. And his nursemaid disappeared at the same time, and I always thought, Miss Dare, that it was the nursemaid who stole him."

"Ransom?" asked Susan.

"No. That was the queer part of it. There never was any attempt to demand ransom. I always felt the nursemaid simply wanted him for herself—she was a very peculiar woman."

Susan brought her gently back to the present.

"So Dixon March is this claimant's name?"

"Yes. That's another thing. It seemed so likely to me that he could remember his name—Derek—and perhaps in saying Derek in his baby way, the people at the orphanage thought it was Dixon he was trying to say, so they called him Dixon. The only trouble is——"

"Yes," said Susan, as Idabelle Lasher's blue eyes wavered and became troubled.

"Well, you see, the other young man, the other Derek—well, his name is Duane. You see?"

Susan felt a little dizzy. "Just what is Dixon's story?"

"He said that he was taken in at an orphanage at the age of six. That he vaguely remembers a woman, dark, with a mole on her chin, which is an exact description of the nursemaid. Of course, we've had the orphanage records examined, but there's nothing conclusive and no way to identify the woman; she died—under the name of Sarah Gant, which wasn't the nursemaid's name—and she was very poor. A social worker simply arranged for the child's entrance into the orphanage."

"What makes him think he is your son, then?"

"Well, it's this way. He grew up and made as much as he could of the education they gave him and actually was making a nice thing with a construction company when he got to looking into his—his origins, he said—and an account of the description of our Derek, the dates, the fact that he could discover nothing of the woman, Sarah Gant, previous to her life in Ottawa——"

"Ottawa?"

"Yes. That was where he came from. The other one, Duane, from New Orleans. And the fact that, as Dixon remembered her, she looked very much like the newspaper pictures of the nursemaid, suggested the possibility that he was our lost child."

"So, on the evidence of corresponding dates and the likeness of the woman who was caring for him before he was taken to the orphanage, comes to you, claiming to be your son. A year after your husband died."

"Yes, and—well——" Mrs. Lasher flushed pinkly. "There are some things he can remember."

"Things—such as what?"

"The—the green curtains in the nursery. There *were* green curtains in the nursery. And a—a calico dog. And—and a few other things. The lawyers say that isn't conclusive. But I think it's very important that he remembers the calico dog."

"You've had lawyers looking into his claims."

"Oh, dear, yes," said Mrs. Lasher. "Exhaustively."

"But can't they trace Sarah Gant?"

"Nothing conclusive, Miss Dare."

"His physical appearance?" suggested Susan.

"Miss Dare," said Mrs. Lasher. "My Derek was blond with gray eyes. He had no marks of any kind. His teeth were still his baby teeth. Any fair young man with gray eyes might be my son. And both these men—either of these men might be Derek. I've looked long and wearily, searching every feature and every expression for a likeness to my boy. It is equally there—and not there. I feel sure that one of them is my son. I am absolutely sure that he has—has come home."

"But you don't know which one?" said Susan softly.

"I don't know which one," said Idabelle Lasher. "But one of them *is Derek*."

She turned suddenly and walked heavily to a window. Her pale green gown of soft crêpe trailed behind her, its hem touching a priceless thin rug that ought to have been in a museum. Behind her, against the gray wall, hung a small Mauve, exquisite. Twenty-one stories below, traffic flowed unceasingly along Lake Shore Drive.

"One of them must be an impostor," Idabelle Lasher was saying presently in a choked voice.

"Is Dixon certain he is your son?"

"He says only that he thinks so. But since Duane has come, too, he is more—more positive——"

"Duane, of course." The rivalry of the two

young men must be rather terrible. Susan had a fleeting glimpse again of what it might mean: one of them certainly an impostor, both impostors, perhaps, struggling over Idabelle Lasher's affections and her fortune. The thought opened, really, quite appalling and horrid vistas.

"What is Duane's story?" asked Susan.

"That's what makes it so queer, Miss Dare. Duane's story—is—well, it is exactly the same."

Susan stared at her wide green back, cushiony and bulgy in spite of the finest corseting that money could obtain.

"You don't mean *exactly* the same!" she cried.

"Exactly," the woman turned and faced her. "Exactly the same, Miss Dare, except for the names and places. The name of the woman in Duane's case was Mary Miller, the orphanage was in New Orleans, he was going to art school here in Chicago when—when, he says, just as Dixon said—he began to be more and more interested in his parentage and began investigating. And he, too, remembers things, little things from his babyhood and our house that only Derek could remember."

"Wait, Mrs. Lasher," said Susan, grasping at something firm. "Any servant, any of your friends, would know these details also."

Mrs. Lasher's pale, big eyes became more prominent.

"You mean, of course, a conspiracy. The lawyers have talked nothing else. But, Miss Dare, they authenticated everything possible to authenticate in both statements. I know what has happened to the few servants we had—all, that is, except the nursemaid. And we don't have many close friends, Miss Dare. Not since there was so much money. And none of them— none of them would do this."

"But both young men can't be Derek," said Susan desperately. She clutched at common sense again and said: "How soon after your husband's death did Dixon arrive?"

"Ten months."

"And Duane?"

"Three months after Dixon."

"And they are both living here with you now?"

"Yes." She nodded toward the end of the long room. "They are in the library now."

"Together?" said Susan irresistibly.

"Yes, of course," said Mrs. Lasher. "Playing cribbage."

"I suppose you and your lawyers have tried every possible test?"

"Everything, Miss Dare."

"You have no fingerprints of the baby?"

"No. That was before fingerprints were so important. We tried blood tests, of course. But they are of the same type."

"Resemblances to you or your husband?"

"You'll see for yourself at dinner tonight, Miss Dare. You will help me?"

Susan sighed. "Yes," she said.

The bedroom to which Mrs. Lasher herself took Susan was done in the French manner with much taffeta, inlaid satinwood, and laced cushions. It was very large and overwhelmingly magnificent, and gilt mirrors reflected Susan's small brown figure in unending vistas.

Susan dismissed the maid, thanked fate that the only dinner gown she had brought was a new and handsome one, and felt very awed and faintly dissolute in a great, sunken, black marble pool that she wouldn't have dared call a tub. After all, reflected Susan, finding that she could actually swim a stroke or two, thirty millions was thirty millions.

She got into a white chiffon dress with silver

and green at the waist, and was stooping in a froth of white flounces to secure the straps of her flat-heeled silver sandals when Mrs. Lasher knocked.

"It's Derek's baby things," she said in a whisper and with a glance over her fat white shoulder. "Let's move a little farther from the door."

They sat down on a cushioned chaise-longue and between them, incongruous against the suave cream satin, Idabelle Lasher spread out certain small objects, touching them lingeringly.

"His little suit—he looked so sweet in yellow. Some pictures. A pink plush teddy bear. His little nursery-school reports—he was already in nursery school, Miss Dare—pre-kindergarten, you know. It was in an experimental stage then, and so interesting. And the calico dog, Miss Dare."

She stopped there, and Susan looked at the faded, flabby calico dog held so tenderly in those fat diamonded hands. She felt suddenly a wave of cold anger toward the man who was not Derek and who must know that he was not Derek. She took the pictures eagerly.

But they were only pictures. One at about

two, made by a photographer; a round baby face without features that were at all distinctive. Two or three pictures of a little boy playing, squinting against the sun.

"Has anyone else seen these things?"

"You mean either of the two boys—either Dixon or Duane? No, Miss Dare."

"Has anyone at all seen them? Servants? Friends?"

Idabelle's blue eyes became vague and clouded.

"Long ago, perhaps," she said. "Oh, many, many years ago. But they've been in the safe in my bedroom for years. Before that in a locked closet."

"How long have they been in the safe?"

"Since we bought this apartment. Ten—no, twelve years."

"And no one—there's never been anything like an attempted robbery of that safe?"

"Never. No, Miss Dare. There's no possible way for either Dixon or Duane to know of the contents of this box except from memory."

"And Dixon remembers the calico dog?"

"Yes." The prominent blue eyes wavered again, and Mrs. Lasher rose and walked toward the door. She paused then and looked at Susan again.

"And Duane remembers the teddy bear and described it to me," she said definitely and went away.

There was a touch of comedy about it, and, like all comedy, it overlay tragedy.

Left to herself, Susan studied the pictures again thoughtfully. The nursery-school reports, written out in beautiful "vertical" handwriting. *Music:* A good ear. *Memory:* Very good. *Adaptability:* Very good. *Sociability:* Inclined to shyness. *Rhythm:* Poor (advise skipping games at home). *Conduct:* (this varied; with at least once a suggestive blank and once a somewhat terse remark to the effect that there had been considerable disturbance during the half hours devoted to naps and a strong suggestion that Derek was at the bottom of it). Susan smiled there and began to like baby Derek. And it was just then that she found the first indication of an identifying trait. And that was after the heading, *Games.* One report said: Quick. Another said: Mentally quick but does not coördinate muscles well. And a third said, definitely pinning the thing down: Tendency to use left hand which we are endeavoring to correct.

Tendency to use left hand. An inborn tendency, cropping out again and again all through life. In those days, of course, it had been rigidly corrected—thereby inducing all manner of ills, according to more recent trends of education. But was it ever altogether conquered?

Presently Susan put the things in the box again and went to Mrs. Lasher's room. And Susan had the somewhat dubious satisfaction of watching Mrs. Lasher open a delicate ivory panel which disclosed a very utilitarian steel safe set in the wall behind it and place the box securely in the safe.

"Did you find anything that will be of help?" asked Mrs. Lasher, closing the panel.

"I don't know," said Susan. "I'm afraid there's nothing very certain. Do Dixon and Duane know why I am here?"

"No," said Mrs. Lasher, revealing unexpected cunning. "I told them you were a dear friend of Christabel's. And that you were very much interested in their—my—our situation. We talk it over, you know, very frankly, Miss Dare. The boys are as anxious as I am to discover the truth of it."

Again, thought Susan feeling baffled, as the true Derek would be. She followed Mrs.

Lasher toward the drawing room again, prepared heartily to dislike both men.

But the man sipping a cocktail in the doorway of the library was much too old to be either Dixon or Duane.

"Major Briggs," said Mrs. Lasher. "Christabel's friend, Susan, Tom." She turned to Susan. "Major Tom Briggs is our closest friend. He was like a brother to my husband, and has been to me."

"Never a brother," said Major Briggs with an air of gallantry. "Say, rather, an admirer. So this is Christabel's little friend." He put down his cocktail glass and bowed and took Susan's hand only a fraction too tenderly.

Then Mrs. Lasher drifted across the room where Susan was aware of two pairs of black shoulders rising to greet her, and Major Briggs said beamingly:

"How happy we are to have you with us, my dear. I suppose Idabelle has told you of our—our problem."

He was about Susan's height; white-haired, rather puffy under the eyes, and a bit too pink, with hands that were inclined to shake. He adjusted his gold-rimmed eyeglasses, then let them drop the length of their black ribbon and said: "What do you think of it, my dear?"

"I don't know," said Susan. "What do you think?"

"Well, my dear, it's a bit difficult, you know. When Idabelle herself doesn't know. When the most rigid—yes, the most rigid and searching investigation on the part of highly trained and experienced investigators has failed to discover—ah—the identity of the lost heir, how may my own poor powers avail!" He finished his cocktail, gulped, and said blandly: "But it's Duane."

"What——" said Susan.

"I said, it's Duane. He is the heir. Anybody could see it with half an eye. Spittin' image of his dad. Here they come now."

They were alike and yet not alike at all. Both were rather tall, slender, and well made. Both had medium-brown hair. Both had grayish-blue eyes. Neither was particularly handsome. Neither was exactly unhandsome. Their features were not at all alike in bone structure, yet neither had features that were in any way distinctive. Their description on a passport would not have varied by a single word. Actually they were altogether unlike each other.

With the salad Major Briggs roused to point out a portrait that hung on the opposite wall.

"Jeremiah Lasher," he said, waving a pink hand in that direction. He glanced meaningly at Susan and added: "Do you see any resemblance, Miss Susan? I mean between my old friend and one of these lads here."

One of the lads—it was Dixon—wriggled perceptibly, but Duane smiled.

"We are not at all embarrassed, Miss Susan," he said pleasantly. "We are both quite accustomed to this sort of scrutiny." He laughed lightly, and Idabelle smiled, and Dixon said:

"Does Miss Dare know about this?"

"Oh, yes," said Idabelle, turning as quickly and attentively to him as she had turned to Duane. "There's no secret about it."

"No," said Dixon somewhat crisply. "There's certainly no secret about it."

There was, however, no further mention of the problem of identity during the rest of the evening. Indeed, it was a very calm and slightly dull evening except for the affair of Major Briggs and the draft.

That happened just after dinner. Susan and Mrs. Lasher were sitting over coffee in the drawing room, and the three men were presumably lingering in the dining room.

It had been altogether quiet in the drawing room, yet there had not been audible even the distant murmur of the men's voices. Thus the queer, choked shout that arose in the dining room came as a definite shock to the two women.

It all happened in an instant. They hadn't themselves time to move or inquire before Duane appeared in the doorway. He was laughing but looked pale.

"It's all right," he said. "Nothing's wrong."

"*Duane*," said Idabelle Lasher gaspingly. "*What*——"

"Don't be alarmed," he said swiftly. "It's nothing." He turned to look down the hall at someone approaching and added: "Here he is, safe and sound."

He stood aside, and Major Briggs appeared in the doorway. He looked so shocked and purple that both women moved hurriedly forward, and Idabelle Lasher said: "Here—on the divan. Ring for brandy, Duane. Lie down here, Major."

"Oh, no—no," said Major Briggs stertorously. "No. I'm quite all right."

Duane, however, supported him to the divan, and Dixon appeared in the doorway.

"What happened?" he said.

Major Briggs waved his hands feebly. Duane said:

"The Major nearly went out the window."

"O-h-h-h——" —it was Idabelle in a thin, long scream.

"Oh, it's all right," said Major Briggs shakenly. "I caught hold of the curtain. By God, I'm glad you had heavy curtain rods at that window, Idabelle."

She was fussing around him, her hands shaking, her face ghastly under its make-up.

"But how could you—" she was saying jerkily—"what on earth—how could it have happened——"

"It's the draft," said the Major irascibly. "The confounded draft on my neck. I got up to close the window and—I nearly went out!"

"But how could you——" began Idabelle again.

"I don't know how it happened," said the Major. "Just all at once—" A look of perplexity came slowly over his face. "Queer," said Major Briggs suddenly, "I suppose it was the draft.

But it was exactly as if——" He stopped, and Idabelle cried:

"As if what?"

"As if someone had pushed me," said the Major.

Perhaps it was fortunate that the butler arrived just then, and there was the slight diversion of getting the Major to stretch out full length on the divan and sip a restorative.

And somehow in the conversation it emerged that neither Dixon nor Duane had been in the dining room when the thing had happened.

"There'd been a disagreement over—well, it was over inheritance tax," said Dixon flushing. "Duane had gone to the library to look in an encyclopedia, and I had gone to my room to get the evening paper which had some reference to it. So the Major was alone when it happened. I knew nothing of it until I heard the commotion in here."

"I," said Duane, watching Dixon, "heard the Major's shout from the library and hurried across."

That night, late, after Major Briggs had gone home, and Susan was again alone in the paralyzing magnificence of the French bedroom, she still kept thinking of the window and Major Briggs. And she put up her own window so circumspectly that she didn't get enough air during the night and woke struggling with a silk-covered eiderdown under the impression that she herself was being thrust out the window.

It was only a nightmare, of course, induced as much as anything by her own hatred of heights. But it gave an impulse to the course she proposed to Mrs. Lasher that very morning.

It was true, of course, that the thing may have been exactly what it appeared to be, and that was, an accident. But if it was not accident, there were only two possibilities.

"Do you mean," cried Mrs. Lasher incredulously when Susan had finished her brief suggestion, "that I'm to say openly that Duane is my son! But you don't understand, Miss Dare. I'm not sure. It may be Dixon."

"I know," said Susan. "And I may be wrong. But I think it might help if you will announce to —oh, only to Major Briggs and the two men— that you are convinced that it is Duane and are taking steps for legal recognition of the fact."

"Why? What do you think will happen? How will it help things to do that?"

"I'm not at all sure it will help," said Susan wearily. "But it's the only thing I see to do. And I think that you may as well do it right away."

"Today?" said Mrs. Lasher reluctantly.

"At lunch," said Susan inexorably. "Telephone to invite Major Briggs now."

"Oh, very well," said Idabelle Lasher. "After all, it will please Tom Briggs. He has been urging me to make a decision. He seems certain that it is Duane."

But Susan, present and watching closely, could detect nothing except that Idabelle Lasher, once she was committed to a course, undertook it with thoroughness. Her fondness for Duane, her kindness to Dixon, her air of relief at having settled so momentous a question, left nothing to be desired. Susan was sure that the men were convinced. There was, to be sure, a shade of triumph in Duane's demeanor, and he was magnanimous with Dixon—as, indeed, he could well afford to be. Dixon was silent and rather pale and looked as if he had not expected the decision and was a bit stunned by it. Major Briggs was incredulous at first, and then openly jubilant, and toasted all of them.

Indeed, what with toasts and speeches on the

part of Major Briggs, the lunch rather prolonged itself, and it was late afternoon before the Major had gone and Susan and Mrs. Lasher met alone for a moment in the library.

Idabelle was flushed and worried.

"Was it all right, Miss Dare?" she asked in a stage whisper.

"Perfectly," said Susan.

"Then—then do you know——"

"Not yet," said Susan. "But keep Dixon here."

"Very well," said Idabelle.

The rest of the day passed quietly and not, from Susan's point of view, at all valuably, although Susan tried to prove something about the possible left-handedness of the real Derek. Badminton and several games of billiards resulted only in displaying the more perfectly a consistent right-handedness on the part of both the claimants.

Dressing again for dinner, Susan looked at herself ruefully in the great mirror.

She had never in her life felt so utterly helpless, and the thought of Idabelle Lasher's faith in her hurt. After all, she ought to have realized her own limits: the problem that Mrs. Lasher had set her was one that would have baffled—that, indeed, had baffled—experts. Who was she, Susan Dare, to attempt its solution?

The course of action she had laid out for Idabelle Lasher had certainly, thus far, had no development beyond heightening an already tense situation. It was quite possible that she was mistaken and that nothing at all would come of it. And if not, what then?

Idabelle Lasher's pale eyes and anxious, beseeching hands hovered again before Susan, and she jerked her satin slip savagely over her head —thereby pulling loose a shoulder strap and being obliged to ring for the maid who sewed the strap neatly and rearranged Susan's hair.

"You'll be going to the party tonight, ma'am?" said the maid in a pleasant Irish accent.

"Party?"

"Oh, yes, ma'am. Didn't you know? It's the Charity Ball. At the Dycke Hotel. In the Chandelier Ballroom. A grand, big party, ma'am. Madame is wearing her pearls. Will you bend your head, please, ma'am."

Susan bent her head and felt her white chiffon being slipped deftly over it. When she emerged she said:

"Is the entire family going?"

"Oh, yes, ma'am. And Major Briggs. There you are, ma'am—and I do say you look beautiful. There's orchids, ma'am, from Mr. Duane. And gardenias from Mr. Dixon. I believe," said the maid thoughtfully, "that I could put them all together. That's what I'm doing for Madame."

"Very well," said Susan recklessly. "Put them all together."

It made a somewhat staggering decoration—staggering, thought Susan, but positively abandoned in luxuriousness. So, too, was the long town car which waited for them promptly at ten when they emerged from the towering apartment house. Susan, leaning back in her seat between Major Briggs and Idabelle Lasher, was always afterward to remember that short ride through crowded, lighted streets to the Dycke Hotel.

No one spoke. Perhaps only Susan was aware (and suddenly realized that she was aware) of the surging desires and needs and feelings that were bottled up together in the tonneau of that long, gliding car. She was aware of it quite suddenly and tinglingly.

Nothing had happened. Nothing, all through

that long dinner from which they had just come, had been said that was at all provocative.

Yet all at once Susan was aware of a queer kind of excitement.

She looked at the black shoulders of the two men, Duane and Dixon, riding along beside each other. Dixon sat stiff and straight; his shoulders looked rigid and unmoving. He had taken it rather well, she thought; did he guess Idabelle's decision was not the true one? Or was he still stunned by it?

Or was there something back of that silence? Had she underestimated the force and possible violence of Dixon's reaction. Susan frowned: it was dangerous enough without that.

They arrived at the hotel. Their sudden emergence from the silence of the car, with its undercurrent of emotion, into brilliant lights and crowds and the gay lilt of an orchestra somewhere, had its customary tonic effect. Even Dixon shook off his air of brooding and, as they finally strolled into the Chandelier Room, and Duane and Mrs. Lasher danced smoothly into the revolving colors, asked Susan to dance.

They left the Major smiling approval and buying cigarettes from a girl in blue pantaloons.

The momentary gayety with which Dixon had asked Susan to dance faded at once. He danced conscientiously but without much spirit and said nothing. Susan glanced up at his face once or twice; his direct, dark blue eyes looked straight ahead, and his face was rather pale and set.

Presently Susan said: "Oh, there's Idabelle!"

At once Dixon lost step. Susan recovered herself and her small silver sandals rather deftly, and Idabelle, large and pink and jewel-laden, danced past them in Duane's arms. She smiled at Dixon anxiously and looked, above her pearls, rather worried.

Dixon's eyebrows were a straight dark line, and he was white around the mouth.

"I'm sorry, Dixon," said Susan. She tried to catch step with him, for the moment, and added: "Please don't mind my speaking about it. We are all thinking of it. I do think you behave very well."

He looked straight over her head, danced several somewhat erratic steps, and said suddenly:

"It was so—unexpected. And you see, I was so sure of it."

"Why were you so sure?" asked Susan.

He hesitated, then burst out again:

"Because of the dog," he said savagely, stepping on one of Susan's silver toes. She removed it with Spartan composure, and he said: "The calico dog, you know. And the green curtains. If I had known there was so much money involved, I don't think I'd have come to—Idabelle. But then, when I did know, and this other—fellow turned up, why, of course, I felt like sticking it out!"

He paused, and Susan felt his arm tighten around her waist. She looked up, and his face was suddenly chalk white and his eyes blazing.

"Duane!" he said hoarsely. "I hate him. I could kill him with my own hands."

The next dance was a tango, and Susan danced it with Duane. His eyes were shining, and his face flushed with excitement and gayety.

He was a born dancer, and Susan relaxed in the perfect ease of his steps. He held her very closely, complimented her gracefully, and talked all the time, and for a few moments Susan merely enjoyed the fast swirl of the lovely Argentine dance. Then Idabelle and Dixon went past, and Susan saw again the expression of Dixon's set white face as he looked at Duane, and Idabelle's swimming eyes above her pink face and bare pink neck.

The rest of what was probably a perfect dance was lost on Susan, busy about certain concerns of her own which involved some adjusting of the flowers on her shoulder. And the moment the dance was over she slipped away.

White chiffon billowed around her, and her gardenias sent up a warm fragrance as she huddled into a telephone booth. She made sure the flowers were secure and unrevealing upon her shoulder, steadied her breath, and smiled a little tremulously as she dialed a number she very well knew. It was getting to be a habit—calling Jim Byrne, her newspaper friend, when she herself had reached an impasse. But she needed him. Needed him at once.

"Jim—Jim," she said. "It's Susan. Listen. Get into a white tie and come as fast as you can to the Dycke Hotel. The Chandelier Room."

"What's wrong?"

"Well," said Susan in a small voice. "I've set something going that—that I'm afraid is going to be more than I meant——"

"You're good at stirring up things, Sue," he said. "What's the trouble now?"

"Hurry, Jim," said Susan. "I mean it." She caught her breath. "I—I'm afraid," she said.

His voice changed.

"I'll be right there. Watch for me at the door." The telephone clicked, and Susan leaned rather weakly against the wall of the telephone booth.

She went back to the Chandelier Room. Idabelle Lasher, pink and worried-looking, and Major Briggs and the two younger men made a little group standing together, talking. She breathed a little sigh of relief. So long as they remained together, and remained in that room surrounded by hundreds of witnesses, it was all right. Surely it was all right. People didn't murder in cold blood when other people were looking on.

It was Idabelle who remembered her duties as hostess and suggested the fortune teller.

"She's very good, they say," said Idabelle. "She's a professional, not just doing it for a stunt, you know. She's got a booth in one of the rooms."

"By all means, my dear," said Major Briggs at once. "This way?" She put her hand on his arm and, with Duane at her other side, moved away, and Dixon and Susan followed. Susan cast a worried look toward the entrance. But Jim couldn't possibly get there in less than thirty minutes, and by that time they would have returned.

Dixon said: "Was it the Major that convinced Idabelle that Duane is her son?"

Susan hesitated.

"I don't know," she said cautiously, "how strong the Major's influence has been."

Her caution was not successful. As they left the ballroom and turned down a corridor, he whirled toward her.

"This thing isn't over yet," he said with the sudden savagery that had blazed out in him while they were dancing.

She said nothing, however, for Major Briggs was beckoning jauntily from a doorway.

"Here it is," he said in a stage whisper as they approached him. "Idabelle has already gone in. And would you believe it, the fortune teller charges twenty dollars a throw!"

The room was small: a dining room, probably, for small parties. Across the end of it a kind of tent had been arranged with many gayly striped curtains.

Possibly due to her fees, the fortune teller did

not appear to be very popular; at least, there were no others waiting, and no one came to the door except a bellboy with a tray in his hand who looked them over searchingly, murmured something that sounded very much like Mr. Haymow, and wandered away. Duane sat nonchalantly on the small of his back, smoking. The Major seemed a bit nervous and moved restlessly about. Dixon stood just behind Susan. Odd that she could feel his hatred for the man lolling there in the armchair almost as if it were a palpable, living thing flowing outward in waves. Susan's sense of danger was growing sharper. But surely it was safe—so long as they were together.

The draperies of the tent moved confusedly and opened, and Idabelle stood there, smiling and beckoning to Susan.

"Come inside, my dear," she said. "She wants you, too."

Susan hesitated. But, after all, so long as the three men were together, nothing could happen. Dixon gave her a sharp look, and Susan moved across the room. She felt a slight added qualm when she discovered that in an effort probably to add mystery to the fortune teller's trade, the swathing curtains had been arranged so that one entered a kind of narrow passage among them, which one followed with several turns before arriving at the looped-up curtain which made an entrance to the center of the maze and faced the fortune teller herself.

Susan stifled her uneasiness and sat down on some cushions beside Idabelle. The fortune teller, in Egyptian costume, with French accent and a Sibylline manner began to talk. Beyond the curtains and the drone of her voice Susan could hear little, although once she thought there were voices.

But the thing, when it happened, gave no warning.

There was only, suddenly, a great dull shock of sound that brought Susan taut and upright and left the fortune teller gasping and still and turned Idabelle Lasher's broad pinkness to a queer pale mauve.

"*What was that?*" whispered Idabelle in a choked way.

And the fortune teller cried: "It's a gunshot —out there!"

Susan stumbled and groped through the folds of draperies, trying to find the way through the entangling maze of curtains and out of the tent.

Then all at once they were outside the curtains and staring at a figure that lay huddled on the floor, and there were people pouring in the door from the hall, and confusion everywhere.

It was Major Briggs. And he'd been shot and was dead, and there was no revolver anywhere.

Susan felt ill and faint and after one long look backed away to the window. Idabelle was weeping, her faced blotched. Dixon was beside her, and then suddenly someone from the hotel had closed the door into the corridor. And a bellboy's voice, the one who'd wandered into the room looking for Mr. Haymow, rose shrilly above the tumult.

"Nobody at all," he was saying. "Nobody came out of the room. I was at the end of the corridor when I heard the shot and this is the only room on this side that's unlocked and in use tonight. So I ran down here, and I can swear that nobody came out of the room after the shot was fired. Not before I reached it."

"Was anybody here when you came in? What did you see?" It was the manager, fat, worried, but competently keeping the door behind him closed against further intrusion.

"Just this man on the floor. He was dead already."

"And nobody in the room?"

"Nobody. Nobody then. But I'd hardly got to him before there was people running into the room. And these three women came out of this tent."

The manager looked at Idabelle—at Susan.

"He was with you?" he asked Idabelle.

"Oh, yes, yes," sobbed Idabelle. "It's Major Briggs."

The manager started to speak, stopped, began again:

"I've sent for the police," he said. "You folks that were in his party—how many of you are there?"

"Just Miss Dare and me," sobbed Idabelle. "And—" she singled out Dixon and Duane—"these two men."

"All right. You folks stay right here, will you? And you, too, miss—" indicating the fortune teller— "and the bellboy. The rest of you will go to a room across the hall. Sorry, but I'll have to hold you till the police get here."

It was not well received. There were murmurs of outrage and horrified looks over slender bare backs and the indignant rustle of trailing gowns, but the scattered groups that had pressed into the room did file slowly out again under the firm look of the manager.

The manager closed the door and said briskly:

"Now, if you folks will be good enough to stay right here, it won't be long till the police arrive."

"A doctor," faltered Idabelle. "Can't we have a doctor?"

The manager looked at the sodden, lifeless body.

"You don't want a doctor, ma'am," he said. "What you want is an under——" He stopped abruptly and reverted to his professional suavity. "We'll do everything in our power to save your feelings, Mrs. Lasher," he said. "At the same time we would much appreciate your—er—assistance. You see, the Charity Ball being what it is, we've got to keep this thing quiet." He was obviously distressed but still suave and competent. "Now then," he said, "I've got to make some arrangements—if you'll just stay here." He put his hand on the door knob and then turned toward them again and said quite definitely, looking at the floor: "It would be just as well if none of you were to try to leave."

With that he was gone.

The fortune teller sank down into a chair and said, "Good gracious me," with some emphasis and a Middle-Western accent. The bellboy retired nonchalantly to a corner and stood there, looking very childish in his smart white uniform, but very knowing. And Idabelle Lasher looked at the man at her feet and began to sob again, and Duane tried to comfort her, while Dixon shoved his hands in his pockets and glowered at nothing.

"But I don't see," wailed Idabelle, "how it could have happened!" Odd, thought Susan, that she didn't ask who did it. That would be the natural question. Or why? Why had a man who was—as she had said, like a brother to her—been murdered?

Duane patted Idabelle's heaving bare shoulders and said something soothing, and Idabelle wrung her hands and cried again: "How could it have happened! We were all together—he was not alone a moment———"

Dixon stirred.

"Oh, yes, he was alone," he said. "He wanted a drink, and I'd gone to hunt a waiter."

"And you forget to mention," said Duane icily, "that I had gone with you."

"You left this room at the same time, but that's all I know."

"I went at the same time you did. I stopped to buy cigarettes, and you vanished. I don't know where you went, but I didn't see you again. Not till I came back with the crowd into this room. Came back to find you already here."

"What do you mean by that?" Dixon's eyes were blazing in his white face, and his hands were working. "If you are accusing me of murder, say so straight out like a man instead of an insolent little puppy."

Duane was white, too, but composed.

"All right," he said. "You know whether you murdered him or not. All I know is when I got back I found him dead and you already here."

"*You*——"

"*Dixon!*" cried Idabelle sharply, her laces swirling as she moved hurriedly between the two men. "Stop this! I won't have it. There'll be time enough for questions when the police come. When the police——" She dabbed at her mouth, which was still trembling, and at her chin, and her fingers went on to her throat, groped, closed convulsively, and she screamed: "*My pearls!*"

"Pearls?" said Dixon staring, and Duane darted forward.

"Pearls—they're gone!"

The fortune teller had started upward defensively, and the bellboy's eyes were like two saucers. Susan said:

"They are certainly somewhere in the room, Mrs. Lasher. And the police will find them for you. There's no need to search for them, now."

Susan pushed a chair toward her, and she sank helplessly into it.

"Tom murdered—and now my pearls gone—and I don't know which is Derek, and I—*I don't know what to do*——" Her shoulders heaved, and her face was hidden in her handkerchief, and her corseted fat body collapsed into lines of utter despair.

Susan said deliberately:

"The room will be searched, Mrs. Lasher, every square inch of it—ourselves included. There is nothing," said Susan with soft emphasis. "Nothing that they will miss."

Then Dixon stepped forward. His face was set, and there was an ominous flare of light in his eyes.

He put his hand upon Idabelle's shoulder to

force her to look up into his face, and brushed aside Duane, who had moved quickly forward, too, as if his defeated rival had threatened Idabelle.

"Why—why, Dixon," faltered Idabelle Lasher, "you look so strange. What is it? Don't, my dear, you are hurting my shoulder——"

Duane cried: "Let her alone. Let her alone." And then to Idabelle: "Don't pay any attention to him. He's out of his mind. He's——" He clutched at Dixon's arm, but Dixon turned, gave him one black look, and thrust him away so forcefully that Duane staggered backward against the walls of the tent and clutched at the curtains to save himself from falling.

"Look here," said Dixon grimly to Idabelle, "what do you mean when you say as you did just now, that you don't know which is Derek? What do you mean? You must tell me. It isn't fair. *What do you mean?*"

His fingers sank into her bulging flesh. She stared upward as if hypnotized, choking. "I meant just that, Dixon. I don't know yet. I only said I had decided in order to——"

"In order to what?" said Dixon inexorably.

A queer little tingle ran along Susan's nerves, and she edged toward the door. She must get help. Duane's eyes were strange and terribly bright. He still clutched the garishly striped curtains behind him. Susan took another silent step and another toward the door without removing her gaze from the tableau, and Idabelle Lasher looked up into Dixon's face, and her lips moved flabbily, and she said the strangest thing:

"*How like your father you are, Derek.*"

Susan's heart got up into her throat and left a very curious empty place in the pit of her stomach. She probably moved a little farther toward the door, but was never sure, for all at once, while mother and son stared revealingly and certainly at each other, Duane's white face and queer bright eyes vanished.

Susan was going to run. She was going to fling herself out the door and shriek for help. For there was going to be another murder in that room. There was going to be another murder, and she couldn't stop it, she couldn't do anything, she couldn't even scream a warning. Then Duane's black figure was outlined against the tent again. And he held a revolver in his hand. The fortune teller said: "Oh, my God" and the white streak that had been the bellboy dissolved rapidly behind a chair.

"Call him your son if you want to," Duane said in an odd jerky way, addressing Mrs. Lasher and Derek confusedly. "Then your son's a murderer. He killed Briggs. He hid in the folds of this curtain till—the room was full of people—and then he came out again. He left his revolver there. And here it is. *Don't move.* One word or move out of any of you, and I'll shoot." He stopped to take a breath. He was smiling a little and panting. "Don't move," he said again sharply. "I'm going to hand you over to the police, Mr. *Derek*. You won't be so anxious to say he's your son then, perhaps. It's his revolver. He killed Briggs with it because Briggs favored me. He knew it, and he did it for revenge."

He was crossing the room with smooth steps; holding the revolver poised threateningly, and his eyes were rapidly shifting from one to another. Susan hadn't the slightest doubt that the smallest move would bring a revolver shot crashing through someone's brain. He's going to escape, she thought, he's going to escape. I can't do a thing. And he's mad with rage. Mad with the terrible excitement of having already killed once.

Duane caught the flicker of Susan's eyes. He was near her now, so near that he could have touched her. He cried:

"It's you that's done this! You that advised her! You were on his side! Well——" He'd reached the door now, and there was nothing they could do. He was gloating openly, the way of escape before him. In an excess of dreadful triumphant excitement, he cried: "I'll shoot you first—it's too bad, when you are so pretty. But I'm going to do it." It's the certainty, thought Susan numbly; Idabelle is so certain that Derek is the other one that Duane knows it, too. He knows there's no use in going on with it. And he knew, when I said what I said about the pearls, that I know.

She felt oddly dizzy. Something was moving. Was she going to faint—was she—something *was* moving, and it was the door behind Duane. It was moving silently, very slowly.

Susan steeled her eyes not to reveal that knowledge. If only Idabelle and Derek would not move—would not see those panels move and betray what they had seen.

Duane laughed.

And Derek moved again, and Idabelle tried to thrust him away from her, and Duane's revolver jerked and jerked again, and the door pushed Duane suddenly to one side and there was a crash of glass, and voices and flashing movement. Susan knew only that someone had pinioned Duane from behind and was holding his arms close to his side. Duane gasped, his hand writhed and dropped the revolver.

Then somebody at the door dragged Duane away; Susan realized confusedly that there were police there. And Jim Byrne stood at her elbow. He looked unwontedly handsome in white tie and tails, but very angry. He said:

"Go home, Sue. Get out of here."

It was literally impossible for Susan to speak or move. Jim stared at her as if nobody else was in the room, got out a handkerchief and wiped his forehead with it.

"I've aged ten years in the last five minutes," he said. He glanced around. Saw Major Briggs's body there on the floor—saw Idabelle Lasher and Derek—saw the fortune teller and the bellboy.

"Is that Mrs. Jeremiah Lasher over there?" he said to Susan.

Mrs. Lasher opened her eyes, looked at him, and closed them again.

Jim looked meditatively at a revolver in his hand, put it in his pocket, and said briskly:

"You can stay for a while, Susan. Until I hear the whole story. Who shot Major Briggs?"

Susan's lips moved and Derek straightened up and cried:

"Oh, it's my revolver all right. But I didn't kill Major Briggs—I don't expect anyone to believe me, but I didn't."

"He didn't," said Susan wearily. "Duane killed Major Briggs. He killed him with Derek's revolver, perhaps, but it was Duane who did the murder."

Jim did not question her statement, but Derek said eagerly:

"How do you know? Can you prove it?"

"I think so," said Susan. "You see, Duane had a revolver when I danced with him. It was in his pocket. That's when I phoned for you, Jim. But I was too late."

"But how——" said Jim.

"Oh, when Duane accused Derek, he actually described the way he himself murdered Major Briggs and concealed himself and the revolver in the folds of the tent until the room was full of people and he could quietly mingle with them as if he had come from the hall. We were all staring at Major Briggs. It was very simple. Duane had got hold of Derek's revolver and knew it would be traced to Derek and the blame put upon him, since Derek had every reason to wish to revenge himself upon Major Briggs."

Idabelle had opened her eyes. They looked a bit glassy but were more sensible.

"Why—" she said— "why did Duane kill Major Briggs?"

"I suppose because Major Briggs had backed him. You see," said Susan gently, "one of the claimants had to be an impostor and a deliberate one. And the attack upon Major Briggs last night suggested either that he knew too much or was a conspirator himself. The exact coinciding of the stories (particularly clever on Major Briggs's part) and the fact that Duane turned up after Major Briggs had had time to search for someone who would fulfill the requirements necessary to make a claim to being your son, seemed to me an indication of conspiracy; besides, the very nature of the case involved imposture. But there had to be a conspiracy; someone had to tell one of the claimants about the things upon which to base his claim, especially about the memories of the baby things—the calico dog," said Susan with a little smile, "and the plush teddy bear. It had to be someone who had known you long ago and could have seen those things before you put them away in the safe. Someone who knew all your circumstances."

"You mean that Major Briggs planned Duane's claim—planned the whole thing? But why——" Idabelle's eyes were full of tears again.

"There's only one possible reason," said Susan. "He must have needed money very badly, and Duane, coming into thirty millions of dollars, would have been obliged to share his spoils."

"Then Derek—I mean Dixon—I mean," said Idabelle confusedly, clutching at Derek, "this one. He really is my son?"

"You know he is," said Susan. "You realized it yourself when you were under emotional stress and obliged to feel instead of reason about it. However, there's reason for it, too. *He is Derek.*"

"He—is—Derek," said Idabelle catching at Susan's words. "You are sure?"

"Yes," said Susan quietly. "He is Derek. You see, I'd forgotten something. Something physical that never changes all through life. That is, a sense of rhythm. Derek has no sense of rhythm and has never had. Duane was a born dancer."

Idabelle said: "Thank God!" She looked at Susan, looked at Derek, and quite suddenly became herself again. She got up briskly, glanced at Major Briggs's body, said calmly: "We'll try to keep some of this quiet. I'll see that things are done decently—after all, poor old fellow, he did love his comforts. Now, then. Oh, yes, if someone will just see the manager of the hotel about my pearls——"

Susan put a startled hand to her gardenias.

"I'd forgotten your pearls, too. Here they are." She fumbled a moment among the flowers, detached a string of flowing beauty, and held it toward Idabelle. "I took them from Duane while we were dancing."

"Duane," said Idabelle. "But——" She took the pearls and said incredulously: "They *are* mine!"

"He had taken them while he danced with you. During the next dance you passed me, and I saw that your neck was bare."

Jim turned to Susan.

"Are you sure about that, Susan?" he said.

"I've managed to get the outline of the story, you know. And I don't think the false claimant would have taken such a risk. Not with thirty millions in his pocket, so to speak."

"Oh, they were for the Major," said Susan. "At least, I think that was the reason. I don't know yet, but I think we'll find that he was pretty hard pressed for cash and had to have some right away. Immediately. Duane probably balked at demanding money of Mrs. Lasher so soon, so the Major suggested the pearls. And Duane was in no position to refuse the Major's demands. Then, you see, he had no pearls because I took them; he and the Major must have quarreled, and Duane, who had already forseen that he would be at Major Briggs's mercy as long as the Major lived, was already prepared for any opportunity to kill him. After he had once got to Idabelle, he no longer needed the Major. He had armed himself with Derek's revolver after what must have seemed to him a heaven-sent chance to stage an accident had failed. Mrs. Lasher's decision removed any remaining small value that the Major was to him and made Major Briggs only a menace. But I think he wasn't sure just what he would do or how—he acceded to the Major's demand for the pearls because it was at the moment the simplest course. But he was ready and anxious to kill him, and when he knew that the pearls had gone from his pocket he must have guessed that I had taken them. And he decided to get rid of Major Briggs at once, before he could possibly tell anything, for any story the Major chose to tell would have been believed by Mrs. Lasher. Later, when I said that the police would search the room, he knew that I knew. And that I knew the revolver was still here."

"Is that why you advised me to announce my decision that Duane was my son?" demanded Idabelle Lasher.

Susan shuddered and tried not to look at that black heap across the room.

"No," she said steadily. "I didn't dream of—murder. I only thought that it might bring the conspiracy that evidently existed somewhere into the open."

Jim said: "Here are the police."

Queer, thought Susan much later, riding along the Drive in Jim's car, with her white chiffon flounces tucked in carefully, and her green velvet wrap pulled tightly about her throat against the chill night breeze, and the scent of gardenias mingling with the scent of Jim's cigarette—queer how often her adventures ended like this: driving silently homeward in Jim's car.

She glanced at the irregular profile behind the wheel and said: "I suppose you know you saved my life tonight."

His mouth tightened in the little glow from the dashlight. Presently he said:

"How did you know he had the pearls in his pocket?"

"Felt 'em," said Susan. "And you can't imagine how terribly easy it was to take them. In all probability a really brilliant career in picking pockets was sacrificed when I was provided with moral scruples."

The light went to yellow and then red, and Jim stopped. He turned and gave Susan a long look through the dusk, and then slowly took her hand in his own warm fingers for a second or two before the light went to green again.

**THE END**